T0317921

24 HOURS IN THE
VIKING WORLD

Also in this series:

24 HOURS IN THE
VIKING
WORLD

A DAY IN THE LIFE
OF THE PEOPLE
WHO LIVED THERE

KIRSTEN WOLF

Michael O'Mara Books Limited

First published in Great Britain in 2024 by
Michael O'Mara Books Limited
9 Lion Yard
Tremadoc Road
London SW4 7NQ

A CIP catalogue record for this book is available from the British Library.

This product is made of material from well-managed, FSC®-certified forests and other controlled sources. The manufacturing processes conform to the environmental regulations of the country of origin.

ISBN: 978-1-78929-583-2 in hardback print format
ISBN: 978-1-78929-584-9 in ebook format

2 3 4 5 6 7 8 9 10

Jacket design and illustration © Patrick Knowles
Designed and typeset by D23
All maps drawn by David Woodroffe
Printed and bound by CPI Group (UK) Ltd, Croydon, CR0 4YY

www.mombooks.com

CONTENTS

Acknowledgements

The best part of finishing a book project is to acknowledge those who have been of assistance. First of all, I want to thank Ross Hamilton for inviting me to undertake the project and for his guidance. I also want to acknowledge Lucy Stewardson's superb editing. Wayne Brabender, my friend, not only read through and edited each chapter, but he also listened patiently to my gripes about the more challenging ones. Laura Moquin and Emily Beyer, both PhD students here at the University of Wisconsin–Madison, were enormously helpful when it came to finding information on a variety of topics covered in this book.

INTRODUCTION

This book takes place in the Viking Age, which, broadly speaking, spans the period 800–1100. The focus is primarily on mainland Scandinavia (Denmark, Norway, Sweden) and Iceland. During these three centuries, Iceland was fully settled and Scandinavia underwent major changes: the modern kingdoms of Denmark, Norway and Sweden took shape, the first towns were established and the pagan Scandinavian religion was gradually abandoned in favour of Christianity. Moreover, the Viking Age witnessed rapid technological developments. It was during that time that bridges and fortresses, such as the ring forts – the most famous being Trelleborg in Denmark – were built. Great advances were also made in shipbuilding and navigation, which enabled the Scandinavians to travel long distances and spread wider in the world than any other European people had done and would do until the voyages and colonizations that followed in the wake of the discoveries of Columbus.

In the course of the Viking Age, the world of the Scandinavians greatly increased in size, and by necessity the

A GLOBE SHOWING THE VAST AREA OF VIKING OCCUPATION, INCLUDING NOT
ONLY SCANDINAVIA BUT ALSO THE SOUTHERN PART OF GREENLAND AND
TODAY'S NEWFOUNDLAND.

picture that is presented of them in this book includes only a
fraction of that world, for it must be recognized that the life
of a Viking marauder was quite different from that of a baker,
shipbuilder or housewife. Also, it must be borne in mind that
there were local variations in terms of lifestyle and professions.
Scandinavia – in the somewhat broader meaning of the word
– is a vast area. It runs from 55° north into the Arctic Ocean,
a distance of more than 2,000km (1,200 miles), and from the
western tip of Iceland at 24° west of Greenwich to the eastern
border of Norway and Finland at 31° east.

Geographically and climatologically, the countries are very different. Denmark is flat, and much of the country is a patchwork of white coastal beaches, blue lakes and green fields. About two thirds of Norway consists of high mountains, and large areas of the rugged mountains are bare rock. The northern part of Sweden is mountainous, whereas the central and southern parts consist of lowlands and highlands. Iceland is a volcanic island. The land is a plateau with mountain peaks and ice fields. The interior consists of glaciers and wasteland.

As a people, the Scandinavians were mostly homogenous at the beginning of the Viking Age, but due to Viking raids and trade – including the import of slaves to Scandinavia, especially from Ireland – there must have been an increasing mixture of races and cultures. Today, one look at Scandinavians who consider themselves indigenous to the region shows people not only with fair hair and blue eyes but also with dark hair and brown eyes. It is important to note that not all Scandinavians were Vikings. The word Viking refers to a vocation and not an ethnic identity. There is, for example, no such thing as a Viking child or a Viking woman. Only a small number of men living in Scandinavia or the Norse islands engaged in Viking activity. The vast majority of men were ordinary and peaceful farmers, fishermen, hunters, merchants, craftsmen, carpenters, blacksmiths or shipbuilders. Some of them also worked as lawyers, peacemakers, poets and rune-carvers. In addition, being a Viking seems mostly to have been a voluntary occupation or profession. It was an opportunity for a young man to get away from home, see and experience parts of the world and make some money – a bit like what attracts some young people to miliary service today.

24 Hours in the Viking World aims to portray the everyday life of Scandinavians and Icelanders and bring these people vividly to life, using information from archaeological research and medieval literary sources. The individual chapters bounce between Denmark, Norway, Sweden, Iceland and the Orkney Islands, and a couple shoot tangents out to Greenland and North America, which the Norse people attempted to colonize. Most of the chapters, however, are set in Iceland, which has the richest medieval literature in terms of describing daily life. The stories are based on actual events, and most of them deal with real and well-known characters, such as King Hakon the Good Haraldsson of Norway, the outlaw Gisli Sursson, the poet Egil Skallagrimsson, and the Viking Svein Asleifarson. A few of the characters are fictional, however, such as the baker Harald Jensson, the housewife Sigrid Steingrimsdottir and the shipbuilder Grim Haraldsson; unfortunately, people in those professions tend not to be featured in the medieval literature. Moreover, to stitch together the often fragmentary archaeological and literary evidence, the biographies of various people are on occasion enhanced by other evidence to provide a coherent narrative. Finally, it should be noted that quite a bit of creative licence has been allowed here and there.

A FARMER IS
MURDERED IN HIS BED

Gisli Sursson lies to his wife, Aud, that he has forgotten to feed one of his guest's horses and needs to go outside for a while. He asks her to bolt the door, then stay awake so she can let him in again when he returns. He takes his spear, Grey-side, from his trunk, puts on a dark cloak over his shirt and his linen underbreeches, and begins to walk towards the stream that runs between his farm at Hol and the farm, Saebol, in the Western Fjords of Iceland. The farm is owned by Thorgrim, his brother-in-law. The stream is the source of water for both farms. Though the water is frigid this night, he wades through it until he reaches the path that leads to Saebol. Gisli does not like what he has set out to do, but he is certain that he must complete his task. His deep feelings of honour leave him no choice.

Special weapons often bore distinguished names relating to their provenance or qualities as a weapon. Examples from Old Norse-Icelandic literature are Leg-biter, Grettir's gift, Battle-flame, Byrnie-biter and Truce-breaker.

Gisli thinks back to the time when he and the other people from Haukadale sat in complete amity at a drinking bout, with plenty of ale and food amid much cheering and sharing of stories, jokes and laughing. Even during that time of amity and peace, however, soothsayer Gest, a wise man whom Gisli highly respects and trusts, warned him that in a few years, not everyone in the group would be in such complete accord. Gisli had been well aware of tensions among the people of Haukadale – after all, what family does not have its disagreements? – but he was surprised to learn how dangerous these differences would become.

The soothsayer's forebodings were often accurate, and Gest's prediction left Gisli desperate for solutions that might change the outcome. Determined to do everything he could, he suggested that he and his kinsmen enter a pact of sworn brotherhood to confirm and seal the solidarity among them. The brotherhood was to include four men: Gisli himself; Gisli's brother Thorkel; their brother-in-law Thorgrim, husband to their sister Thordis; and Vestein, brother to Gisli's wife, Aud. While naming all the gods as their witnesses, Gisli proposed that the four of them swear an oath to avenge any harm done to those in the brotherhood. All agreed, but when they joined hands Thorgrim suddenly withdrew his hand from Vestein's, saying he only felt obligated to enter into the pact with his wife's brothers, not with Vestein. In response, Gisli declared he was unwilling to undertake any responsibilities on Thorgrim's behalf. It was safe to say the brotherhood had its challenges from the beginning.

As Gest predicted, and much to Gisli's disappointment, any sense of companionship that had once been felt among the four men soon started to deteriorate. Gisli's immediate concern was for the safety of his beloved brother-in-law Vestein, who was setting out on a voyage abroad. So, Gisli went to his smithy and made what looked like a large coin – a one-of-a-kind metal disc, cut into halves that fit together perfectly. Gisli kept one half and gave the other to Vestein before he left. They agreed that if either one ever felt that his life was threatened, he would send his half of the disc to the other as a call for help. Something inside Gisli told him that one day it would come into use.

Some time later, when Gisli and Aud were snuggling in bed, she told him about a conversation she'd had with Asgerd, the wife of his brother Thorkel. Gisli and Thorkel shared a farm, and their wives were close with one another. While the two sisters-in-law weaved and chatted, Aud asked Asgerd if she'd had an affair with Vestein. Asgerd said no but readily confessed that she felt very attracted to Vestein and liked him better than her own husband. To her horror, Aud realized that Thorkel had overheard their conversation. Despite being upset after hearing Aud's story, Gisli did not blame her, for, as he said, 'Someone had to speak the words of fate. What is destined will come to pass.'

Soon after, Thorkel requested that he and Gisli divide their estate. Though Gisli knew he personally would benefit from this arrangement because Thorkel was seldom around the farm, living more like a parasite than a co-owner, he was still opposed to it. His feelings of family integrity were too strong. Without the bonds of common ownership, Gisli feared that the solidarity within their family would become weak. Nonetheless, Thorkel had his way and moved to Saebol, their brother-in-law Thorgrim's farm, a short distance away. By then, it was clear to Gisli that Vestein was in serious danger. Thorkel was still bound by his oath, to be sure, but Thorgrim was free to seek vengeance on his brother-in-law's behalf. So, when Gisli learned that Vestein had returned to Iceland from his voyage, he sent messengers to him with his half of the metal disc – but Vestein took a different route from that the messengers expected, and Gisli had no means of tracking him down.

During the two nights after Vestein's arrival at Hol, Gisli had trouble falling asleep. When eventually he did sleep, he had disturbing dreams that he did not want to reveal to anyone, including his own wife. Gisli was the only one awake on the third night when a strong gust of wind hit the house so hard it took off all the roofing on one side while rain poured outside like never before. Gisli and his farmhands sprung out of their beds to cover the hay in the fields, which left only one farmhand, a slave, Thord the Coward, still inside the house with Vestein and Aud. Vestein offered to help, but Gisli asked him to stay home with his sister.

The roof soon began to leak so badly that Vestein and Aud had to move their beds to drier areas of the house. Then, just before daybreak, Aud awoke to hear Vestein call out, 'Struck there!' She quickly rose and ran to see her brother fall down dead beside his bedpost with a spear through his chest. Although in complete shock at the sight, she managed to compose herself and asked Thord the Coward to remove the weapon, but he refused. He knew that in Iceland whoever draws a weapon from a death wound is obliged to take revenge. He also knew that if the weapon is left in the fatal wound it is considered secret manslaughter, not murder. Just then, Gisli entered and took the spear out of the wound and threw it, dripping with blood, into a trunk so no one else might see it.

Gisli sat down on the edge of the bed to collect his thoughts. Eventually, he decided to send his foster daughter to Saebol to see what was going on there. When she returned, she reported that her welcome had not been warm and that no one at Saebol showed grief or surprise when she told them about Vestein's murder. In fact, Thorgrim was fully armed with his helmet and sword, she said, while Gisli's brother Thorkel was also holding a sword. Gisli was not surprised at the news. He immediately began to prepare a burial mound for Vestein in the sandbank on the far side of the pond below Saebol. Many people attended Vestein's funeral, including Thorkel, who encouraged Gisli not to let Vestein's murder affect him so much that he would consider revenge.

Gisli could not let the matter rest, however. He could not ignore his brotherhood obligation to Vestein, and by extension to Aud, who was taking the death of her brother very hard. Although she did not cry much, Gisli knew his wife well enough to know she was desperately missing her brother. Moreover, he could not forget that he was the one who had drawn the weapon from the death wound; he must take revenge against Vestein's murderer, whom he knew to be Thorgrim. It was his turn to strike back.

In the spring, Gisli and Thorgrim decided to host a feast at their farms to celebrate the end of winter. They invited crowds of people. While decorating his house at Saebol, Thorgrim sent Geirmund, one of his workers, to Hol to retrieve some tapestries Vestein had intended to give as gifts to Thorkel but which Thorkel had refused. Gisli readily agreed to give Geirmund the tapestries and accompanied him as far as the hayfield. It was there that Gisli saw his chance to retaliate against Thorgrim, telling Geirmund that in return for use of the tapestries, he should unbolt three of Saebol's farmhouse doors before he went to bed. Geirmund agreed.

The walls of houses in the Viking Age appear to have been wainscoted, and in some houses the panels were adorned with incized carving or woven hangings or tapestries – narrow strips of cloth with embroidered or woven decoration. The latter, which were a privilege of the wealthier members of society, served the dual purpose of decoration and insulation.

Gisli knows the layout of the farm at Saebol well because he built it himself. There is a door leading into the house from the byre, which is where he decides to enter first. He finds thirty cows standing on each side and ties their tails together so they cannot move, closing the byre door on his way out so it cannot be opened from the inside. He proceeds to the farmhouse and finds that Geirmund has kept his promise: three of the farmhouse doors are unbolted. Gisli quietly walks in and closes the doors behind him. He stands still for a while and listens to see if anyone is awake. Assured that all are asleep, he decides to douse the three lights he finds burning in the farmhouse. He picks up some rushes off the floor and strands them together, softly tossing the bundle at the first light to extinguish it. As he is making another bundle to put out the second light, Gisli freezes. In the dimly lit room, he sees the hand of a young man reach for the third light, take down the lamp-holder and snuff out the flame. It seems like an eternity before Gisli feels safe to go further into the house.

Because of the darkness he has difficulty finding his way, but eventually he finds the bed closet where his sister, Thordis, and Thorgrim tend to sleep. The door to their bed closet is closed. Gisli slowly manages to open it without waking a soul, then can barely make out that both are in their bed. He proceeds quietly and begins to grope under the covers for Thorgrim. It is so dark he does not realize he has touched the breast of Thordis, who is sleeping on the near side of the bed. His touch wakes his sister, who nudges Thorgrim and asks him: 'Why is your hand so cold, Thorgrim?' Thorgrim mumbles and shifts in his sleep.

A RECONSTRUCTED ICELANDIC FARMHOUSE, LOCATED AT
STÖNG, THJORSARDALUR, IN THE CENTRE OF THE COUNTRY.

Gisli fears they can hear his pounding heart, so he waits a little longer and warms his hands inside his tunic. When he is sure they are both asleep again, he reaches over Thordis and lightly touches Thorgrim, who had again turned away from his wife. Thorgrim now stirs, wakes up, and as he turns towards Thordis once again Gisli quickly pulls the bedclothes off the couple with one hand, and with the other plunges Grey-side through Thorgrim's side so hard that the sword sticks fast into the bed. As Gisli quickly and quietly moves back through the house, he locks the doors after him. He can hear Thordis cry out that her husband has been killed.

Snow begins to fall, covering all the paths, and he starts to head home the same way he came. Behind him, he hears the commotion among the inebriated men, who wonder what to do while they trample around in the snow and destroy any footprints Gisli might have left behind. When he arrives back home at Hol, Aud unlocks the door. She asks him no questions. Gisli goes to bed with a good conscience for fulfilling his oath of sworn brotherhood. He falls asleep immediately.

Later, Gisli recited an incriminating stanza that was overheard and interpretated by his sister, the victim's wife:

> *I saw the shoots reach*
> *up through melting frost*
> *on the grim man's mound;*
> *I slew that warrior.*
> *The warrior has slain*
> *that man, and given*
> *one, greedy for new land,*
> *a plot of his own forever.*

The revelation soon led to his long outlawry and eventual death while defending himself against his enemies. It is worth noting that in Iceland, outlawry was the harshest possible punishment. There were two basic types of outlawry, referred to as 'lesser outlawry' and 'full outlawry'. Lesser outlawry was a sentence of a three-year exile from the country. A full outlaw lost all his rights. No one was allowed to help him in any way or give him passage abroad. Anyone could slay him with impunity either in Iceland or abroad.

8TH HOUR OF THE NIGHT
(01.00–02.00)

A SKALD WOUNDED IN
BATTLE IS TREATED BY
A HEALER

It has been a very long, sad and difficult day for Thormod Bersason. Thormod is an Icelandic skald, a composer and reciter of poetry at the court of the Norwegian King Olaf Haraldsson. He is nicknamed Coal-brow's Skald because back home he made love poetry about Thorbjörg Coal-brow. It is late in the evening, and Thormod is emotionally and physically exhausted from having fought in battle – a battle in which his beloved King Olaf has died and Thormod himself has been gravely wounded.

A skald is the Old Norse-Icelandic term for a poet. The noun is typically used about poets who composed skaldic poetry, an intricate form of verse. It took a long training to become a skald. Skalds were often hired by Scandinavian royals to compose verses in memory of their victories or defeats and to provide entertainment. The rewards for poetry were hospitality and gifts of treasure.

Like many others on the defeated side, Thormod had retreated from where he and his companions thought the greatest danger lay. Some members of the army fled running, but fatigued and wounded from fighting Thormod could do nothing except stand near his comrades at what he thought was a safe distance and watch the carnage unfold. All of a sudden, he was struck by an arrow in his left side. Breaking off the shaft with a stifled cry, he left the battle and ventured in search of lodging and assistance.

By now it is late in the evening, Thormod is dragging himself along, and all he has is a bare sword in his hand. It is not particularly cold, but it is raining, the path is muddy, and he is not at all familiar with the area. He is filthy, sweaty, and his torn clothes are soaked with blood. On his way, he is haunted by the horrors he witnessed and experienced during the day. Because of his disproportionately small army, King Olaf had not fared well, although in Thormod's view he defended himself courageously. At the battle's climax, a man by the name of Thorstein Shipbuilder had hacked at King

Olaf with his battleaxe, and the blow struck his left leg below the knee. After receiving the wound, which almost severed his leg, the king leaned against a boulder, unable to stand. Despite the blood pouring down onto his foot, King Olaf did not flinch, but taking advantage of the king's injury and immobilization a man by the name of Thorir the Hound thrust at him with his spear, piercing him below his coat of mail and through the belly. Finally, a certain Kalf slashed at the king, the blow striking his neck on the left side. No one could survive such wounds, but to see King Olaf fall was a shock to all. Men screamed at the sight of their slain leader – and yet they kept fighting.

Thormod is still in shock as he reflects on the events that led to this moment. King Olaf had recently returned from exile in Russia to reclaim the throne in Norway, but some of the powerful chieftains became angry with him due to his violent behaviour. Joining forces with King Cnut the Great of Denmark and his Norwegian vassal, Earl Hakon Eiriksson, they had expelled King Olaf from his domain. The exiled king was staying with Grand Duke Yaroslav of Novgorod, where he received the news that Earl Hakon had been drowned. Sensing an opportunity to reclaim his crown, Olaf decided to leave his asylum. He was aware he would likely meet with resistance, so while travelling through Sweden he set about raising an army of approximately 480 men. In Norway, he found an additional group of supporters, extending to approximately 3,000 men. Olaf had not anticipated, however, that he would be fighting against a much larger army raised by Norwegian chieftains, numbering some 14,000 peasants.

The night before the battle, just outside the village of Stiklestad, King Olaf slept briefly and fitfully surrounded by his men. He awakened just as the sun was rising and called for Thormod, asking his skald to recite a poem for the army. Gathering himself, Thormod closed his eyes, took a deep breath and recited the poem 'The Old Lay of Bjarki', an incitement to battle. His voice rang out so clearly and loudly that the entire army awoke. Impressed with the poem, the troops had decided to call it 'Housecarls' Exhortation'.

From 'The Old Lay of Bjarki':
Day has broken;
the rooster's feathers rustle;
it is time for the sons of toil to get to work.
Wake now and wake, friends,
all the noblest companions of Adils.

Now trudging along, the battle receding behind him, Thormod eventually finds a large barn. Light flickers within and the sound of voices drifts from inside. He enters and is immediately confronted by a man complaining about all the wailing and lamenting of wounded men strewn about the place. Continuing his rant, the man opines that while maybe King Olaf's men acquitted themselves well in the battle, they are certainly bearing their wounds poorly. Offended, Thormod demands the man's name and asks whether he fought in the battle himself. In return, the man introduces himself as Kimbi and tells Thormod that he had in fact been in the army consisting mostly of peasants. Kimbi then asks if Thormod was in the battle. Thormod replies that he was on the opposite side, the one that defended King Olaf. Tension crackles between the two until, after a few moments have passed, Kimbi offers to hide Thormod in exchange for a gold ring he wears on his arm – a gift from King Olaf – warning him that otherwise the Norwegian peasants will kill him. Despite his exhaustion, Thormod remains clear-minded. The glint in Kimbi's eyes tells him that his would-be saviour has no good intentions. As Kimbi reaches for the ring, Thormod shifts his weight and flashes his sword, severing the man's hand. Kimbi reels backwards and cries out, but no one takes much notice; the hall is littered with men with far worse injuries than his.

Stumbling away from the encounter, Thormod ventures further into the hall and sits down heavily, listening to the conversations about King Olaf and the battle itself. The wounded mostly talk in hushed tones about what they have seen in the battle and discuss how the combatants have fought. Not everyone is quick to praise King Olaf, much to Thormod's displeasure, and he speaks a verse in an attempt to redeem his patron:

Oaken-hearted Olaf
onward strode – blood-covered
steel bit deep at Stiklestad –
and urged his men on.
Shields sheltered all from
shower of arrows – tried was
many a warrior's mettle in
medley – but the leader.

Making little headway, Thormod decides he has had enough of their talk and makes up his mind to go to a small, detached building on the farm. When he enters, he sees many severely injured men, and a woman is among them, busy bandaging their wounds. Thormod is somewhat curious about her ethnic background. From her appearance, he guesses that she is Sámi; he has heard that Sámi women are skilled physicians, though mostly in magic healing. He is too tired from loss of blood and the events of the day to give the idea much thought, but the fact that a female healer is in charge is not surprising.

Medical treatment is typically the province of women in this era. In order to treat their patients, they rely on their own observations, experiences and, not least, health advice passed along by word of mouth from previous generations. Many people would have been quite unfamiliar with medical practices, but stories abounded about herbal remedies, special diets, steam baths, purges, bloodletting (phlebotomy) and surgical intervention.

From back home in Iceland, Thormod also knows that in former times some women practised magical medicine and used charms. He knows that runes, too, may have healing powers. Mind wandering, he recollects a stanza from the poem 'Lay of Sigrdrifa', in which the valkyrie Sigrdrifa provides Sigurd the dragon slayer with runic wisdom.

*Helping-runes you must know if you want to assist
and release children from women;
they shall be cut on the palms and clasped on the joints,
and then the goddesses asked for help.
Limb-runes you must know if you want to be a healer
and know how to see to wounds;
on bark they must be cut and of the tree of the wood,
on those whose branches bend east.*

In fact, he now vaguely remembers a story he had heard in Iceland about a man by the name of Egil Skallagrimsson, who used runes to cure a 'wasting sickness'. According to the story, Egil had been visiting with a farmer whose young daughter was very ill. He had ordered the patient to be lifted out of her bed and placed on clean sheets. Examining the bed, Egil had found a whalebone with runes carved on it by the farmer's son, who had previously tried to cure her, though upon inspection he realized the runes were incorrectly executed. Egil had shaved the runes off into the fire to render them powerless and had the patient's bedclothes aired before reinscribing some runes and placing the new inscriptions under the pillow of the bed where she was lying. Soon she had begun to recover.

A fire burns on the floor of the small building, and the woman healer is heating water for cleansing the injured men's wounds. Thormod decides to sit down near the door, where he can watch other people attending to the wounded walking in and out. One of these people notices that Thormod is very pale and asks him why he does not request help from the healer himself. Thormod replies in verse that he has been wounded by an arrow and gets up to stand before the fire. After a short while, the healer woman, not noticing the severity of his condition, tells him to go outside and bring her some firewood to heat more water. Thormod complies, and when he comes back in she too notices his pallor and questions him. Again, Thormod replies in verse, in which he tries to explain to her that an arrow has hit him close to his heart:

The woman wonders, why so
the condition of the warrior.
Few from wounds become fair-hued;
the flight of arrows found me.
The ice-cold iron, woman,
flew through my middle.
Hard by my heart, I think,
the baleful weapon hit me.

The woman demands to see his injuries, so Thormod removes his clothes. While inspecting his wounds, she looks very closely at the gash in his side. Concerned, she notices that there is iron in it, but she cannot determine which path the arrow has taken. She swiftly sets about making a concoction, a sort of test meal, in a stone kettle in which she mashes leeks and other local herbs and boils them together. Thormod does not know what kind of herbs she is using, but he thinks that they may be a combination of mugwort (plantain), stime (watercress), atterlothe, maythem (camomile), nettle, crab-apple, chervil and fennel.

Healers often gave this meal to wounded men.
In this way, they could determine if they had wounds
in vital internal organs, because the scent of the leek
and herbs might permeate through a wound that went
into the body cavity. The technique was passed down
from mothers and grandmothers.

She brings some of this concoction to Thormod, but he flatly refuses to eat it and tells her that he is not porridge-sick. He realizes that she probably did not understand his Icelandic verse, knowing very well that the wound is in his heart and not in his stomach. The skald insists on a surgical approach, and the healer accordingly takes a pair of pincers and tries to pull out the head of the arrow – but it is stuck fast and will not budge. The protruding arrowhead hardly shows because the wound is so swollen. Thormod tells the healer to make a cut, so the iron can be reached with the pincers, but she is not at all used to doing surgery and feels nervous about the task.

VIKING AGE ARM RINGS LIKE THE ONE GIVEN TO THORMOD.

Thormod understands and appreciates that she is at least attempting to help him. He wants to reward her for her service, so he gives her the gold ring on his arm – the only thing of value he has – and tells her to do with it as she pleases. The healer is deeply grateful; she is not used to being compensated for her service and she is not wealthy. Moreover, she has a large family to feed back at home. Feeling a calm wash over him, Thormod takes the pincers himself and pulls out the arrowhead. He looks at it and sees that it has barbs on it, and that there are fibres of his heart in it, some red and some white. He comments that this is a sign that King Olaf fed his men well, because there is still fat around the roots of his heart. He leans back, at peace with the inevitability of his death, and a moment later he is dead.

Thormod would never know that this battle, the Battle of Stiklestad, which took place on 29 July 1030, would become the most famous land battle in Viking Age Norway. Moreover, he would never know that his verses would be remembered and that a couple of centuries later historian Snorri Sturluson would include some of them in his telling of the Battle of Stiklestad in his famous work *Heimskringla*. The skald is at rest, but his words live on.

9TH HOUR OF THE NIGHT
(02.00–03.00)

A WOMAN GIVES BIRTH

Signy Valbrandsdottir lies on a bed of straw on the floor in some small building next to the farmhouse in Reykjadale. The pain of her contractions has left her so delirious that she does not know if she is in the animal shed or the barn. She is aware that she is surrounded by several women, all servants, including two from the farm. She feels the urge to call out to her foster mother Thordis, a skilled and practical woman. They had always been close. Sadly, Thordis had died, suddenly and of unknown causes, only a few months earlier. But now a kind and elderly woman, whom Signy believes to be a local midwife, begins to examine her. The woman presses her hands on Signy's belly here and there to make sure the baby has dropped enough that she can start an internal examination. She gently probes inside Signy's vagina, then assures her that she is fully dilated, that she can feel the baby's head and that, despite the severe pain in her back, this is not a breech birth.

'The baby will be born very soon,' she says. 'You must push and take deep breaths with each contraction.'

The controlled breathing helps relieve her pain a little. One of the women soothes her forehead with a damp cloth dipped into a small cauldron of cold water. Another holds her hand, which Signy clenches every time she has another contraction. The mother-to-be continues to push and push, but the baby will not come. She begins to worry that maybe her baby is too big, as she had expected to give birth a couple of weeks earlier.

'Stop pushing,' the midwife says suddenly.

'I can't stop,' Signy moans. 'I can't.'

'We'll help you,' says the midwife. She and the other women shift Signy to a knee-and-elbow position. Two women support her elbows and others sit at her knees, while the midwife places herself to receive the baby from behind. Signy now hears the midwife chanting. She wonders if it is a magical formula or a song. She knows that chants are used to invoke the fertility goddesses Frigg and Freyja and sometimes used as remedies for difficult births.

Signy is now beyond exhaustion. Her long day had started outside doing farm chores. It was then she first felt cramping in her lower stomach, not unlike her monthly period pains. A little later, she developed a dull lower back ache, and then a pain in her inner thighs that went down her legs. She soon noticed some spotting, so she returned to the farmhouse for her menstrual cloth, which she put between her legs before continuing to work outside. The work distracted her from her labour, and besides, the midsummer evening had turned beautiful. Sometimes she had to sit down or squat until her contractions eased, but at least she could appreciate the view in such moments.

When her bleeding increased and her pain became intolerable, she once again returned to the farmhouse. By then it was late evening. Servants offered her some food, but she told them she was not hungry. In fact, she'd had no appetite and had eaten only small meals for days. The people at the farm asked her to lie down and rest, while her contractions kept getting stronger and more frequent. After midnight, when the sun began to rise, she felt warm liquid gushing from between her legs. Realizing that her water had broken, she asked the servant women for help. They immediately led her to the outside building where she could have her privacy.

Though Signy is feeling scared now, this is not her first pregnancy or birth. She has one son, Grim, from her marriage to her late husband Thorgeir of Midfell. That birth had not been difficult at all, but she had been younger then. Also, she had later given birth to a boy, whom her second husband, Grimkel Bjarnarson, had named Hörd. That delivery, too, had gone well. Though Hörd would grow up to be strong, he had not been well developed at first. At age three, he still could not walk by himself. When Hörd was four, his father, a devout heathen, had decided to preside over a sacrifice at their farm at Ölfusvatn.

During the event's preparation, Signy had been inside, getting ready and trying to make herself look beautiful for the guests who had been invited. She was seated with her fine pendant on her lap, while Hörd stood by a bench along the wall. For the first time in his life, he took a few steps by himself towards his mother, but then he stumbled into her knees, inadvertently grabbing the pendant and throwing it to the floor, where it shattered into tiny pieces. Furious, Signy began to scold Hörd, just as her husband walked into the room. Grimkel angrily picked up his son and took him to two friends, requesting that they raise Hörd. Signy was devastated both by the removal of her son and by the destruction of her pendant but later realized that Grimkel could not have known the stone was a birth adjuvant – a stone worn as an amulet by pregnant and parturient women.

Signy has not seen Hörd since he was taken away from her. Without her good-luck amulet, she has become deeply concerned that maybe she will give birth to a deformed baby. The matter of the broken stone has been on her mind throughout her pregnancy, which, unlike her previous two pregnancies, has been different, unpleasant. She had felt terribly nauseous and tired, especially during the first trimester. She struggled to keep food down. And now she finds herself away from her home at Ölfusvatn and away from her husband, though she realizes he would be of little use in this situation. She knows that most men prefer not to get involved when a woman gives birth. They consider childbirth 'a woman's business'.

In some ways, she is also grateful that he is not here as she had been married to Grimkel against her will. Grimkel had approached her father, Valbrand, at the Thing, the voting assembly of freemen, to ask for her hand in marriage, and her father had agreed.

The main legislative and judicial assembly in medieval Iceland was the Althing, which was established in 930. It united all regions of the country under a common legal and judicial system, without depending upon the executive power of a monarch or regional rulers. The Althing met for two weeks every summer at Thingvellir in south-western Iceland. In addition, there were regional and local Things, with the latter convoked for special ends.

When Valbrand returned from the Thing and told Signy and her brother, Torfi, the news, Torfi had words with their father. He did not consider Signy's arranged marriage to be worthy. He called Grimkel old and tyrannical and predicted that the marriage would not bring her happiness. Later, Torfi told Signy that he did not want her to marry out of the district and take her property away, but she asked him not to break up the engagement. She promised that she would hand all her property over to him so he could pay the dowry their father had agreed on. She assured Torfi that there would be plenty of money left for him. She only asked to keep the two treasures she valued most: her pendant and her horse, Svartfaxi.

A HERD OF ICELANDIC HORSES. THESE UNUSUAL HORSES ARE OFTEN PONY-SIZED, HAVE LONG LIFESPANS AND ARE AS HARDY AS THEIR ENVIRONMENT DEMANDS.

Though Torfi agreed to all this, he later refused to go on the wedding trip, and their father was too old and feeble to travel as well. So, one of Grimkel's friends, a man named Koll, from Lund, offered to ride at the head of the guest party. It was a long journey, so they spent the night in south Reykjadale. The next morning, Svartfaxi could not be found among the other horses. Following tracks in the dew, one of the men in the party rode north to look over the ridge towards Flokadale. He found Signy's horse dead in an eroded gully in the valley. Signy had lost her favourite horse, one of her two treasures in life, so she insisted on returning home, but Koll refused and the wedding took place regardless. The guests left and only Thordis, her foster mother, stayed behind.

After Grimkel took Hörd away from her, Signy had come to despise him. She could barely stand the sight of him and certainly did not want to become pregnant by him again. She attempted coitus interruptus, but her husband would have none of that. She tried various means of birth control, including inserting lily root and rue into her vagina. Sometimes, when she sensed that her husband was in the mood for sex, she would gather moss to insert as deeply as she could. She was always relieved when she had her period, because then he would leave her alone. Despite her many efforts, however, she eventually became pregnant. In fact, her pregnancy was revealed in a dream, in which she saw a tree with enormous roots and many limbs covered with leaves. She told her foster mother about the dream. Thordis interpreted it to mean that Signy and Gimkel would have a daughter from whom a large family, represented by the roots, would descend. She also said the tree covered with leaves symbolized a religious conversion and that their progeny would follow the faith that would be proclaimed.

Dreams played an important role in medieval Icelandic literature and culture. The significance of dreams was based on the belief that they were infused into the minds of people by supernatural powers. Properly interpreted, they could foretell the future.

Once she knew for certain that she was pregnant, Signy asked Grimkel to let her visit her relatives. He grudgingly allowed it, but only on the condition that she would not be gone longer than two weeks. Two farmhands and Thordis went with her, the four riding north to Reykjadale, where her brother Torfi gave them a warm welcome. He told Signy to ignore Grimkel's demand to return in two weeks. And she did. She enjoyed her time with Torfi so much she decided to stay. It evidently mattered little to Grimkel; he never visited and made no attempt bring her back. Indeed, he would never see her again.

Now Signy pushes and pushes and shakes with fever. Finally, she gives birth to a very large girl. The midwife places the baby on her chest. Signy is impressed with her healthy screams and well-defined muscles. The baby's movements are strong. She already seems aware of her fingers as they move around in the air. Signy is filled with happiness and flooded with relief. She has given birth to a perfectly normal girl.

While Signy nurses the baby girl, who latches on immediately, the midwife cuts the umbilical cord. A man brings in cooled water that has been boiled, which one of the women uses to gently wash the baby. The midwife then begins to massage Signy's belly to remove the placenta, which must come out for Signy to survive.

In Viking Age and Medieval Iceland, some people considered the placenta a fetch, a part of the infant's soul, which was not whole until the placenta had been released. In fact, some people believed that the placenta was a twin brother or sister, who accompanied a man or a woman throughout life and defended them against danger. So, the placenta should be tended to carefully and not thrown out where animals might eat it, or the child would be forever deprived.

The midwife keeps massaging her belly, but the placenta does not release. Signy then feels the nurse reach into her vagina to loosen the placenta. It hurts. It feels as though the midwife's whole arm is inside her. Signy begs her to stop, but the midwife tells her she cannot. She says her placenta is stuck to her uterus, and she can only remove bits and pieces of it at a time. Signy is bleeding heavily and starts to black out. Her vision seems to be going, and everything start to get very blurry. She is unsure if she should try to stay awake or ease into sleep. She drifts in and out. In her lucid moments she wonders if she will see Torfi again, when suddenly he appears. From the expression she can make out on his face, she can tell he is dreadfully worried. She can barely hear him tell the women that he will under no circumstances have the baby sprinkled with water until they know for sure that Signy will live. She is too drained to keep her eyes open any longer and knows she will not live to see the sun rise. She closes them and they never open again.

10TH HOUR OF THE NIGHT
(03.00–04.00)

A BAKER STARTS
MAKING BREAD

Harald Jensson wakes up and lies quietly in his bed waiting for his neighbour's rooster to crow. The rooster begins to crow at exactly 3 a.m. every day during the summer, when the sun rises early. Harald always enjoys these last few minutes in bed, where it is warm and cozy. He knows that he has a busy day ahead because two trading ships arrived last evening, and he expects a lot of business from hungry crew members wanting fresh bread after many days spent on a ship eating mouldy baked goods.

Harald was born and raised here in Hedeby, and over the years he has seen it prosper and grow as a trading centre. Traders now come from all over, though mostly from Germany and the Baltic. He knows that the reason for Hedeby's success is its geographical location on the neck of the Jutland Peninsula near the Schlei fjord, from which rivers flow into the Eider and the North Sea. He considers himself very lucky to live there. Because Hedeby is enclosed by a semi-circular rampart on three sides – north, west and south – he has always felt safe from attacks. To the east, it is open to Haddeby Nor, an inlet of the Schlei that provides a sheltered harbour, as well as access to the fjord. That rampart is then connected to Danevirke, a system of earthworks protecting the Danish border by a connecting wall.

Most of his customers come from Germany. Harald has no problem understanding them, because he has lived so close to Germany all his life that he is virtually bilingual. But other customers come to his bakery speaking languages he does not know, so they must communicate together through hand gestures. A customer points at what he wants to purchase and how many, then Harald uses his fingers to indicate the price. When it comes time for payment, Scandinavian traders tend to use coins struck in Hedeby. These anonymous imitations of French *deniers* are minted in the Fristian town of Dorestad. Some of these coins have an abbreviated form of Carolus (Holy Roman Emperor Charlemagne) and Dorestad on their surface, while others are stamped with animals, ships and the like. Some of the foreign customers use Kufic coins minted in the Abbasid and Samanid Caliphate. These coins typically have text quotations from the Quran on their faces, though when they circulate among locals Harald has on occasion seen Thor's hammers or crosses scratched into the surface over the text.

Weighing scales were used by tradesmen for taking payments in the Viking Age.

Regardless of what coins the customers use, Harald examines them carefully to make sure they are made of pure silver. To weigh them, he uses a small scale formed of two bronze pans, which hang from a bronze arm, one pan at each end, suspended by thin chains. To balance the scale, he has his choice of seven lead weights, some of which are topped with cut-up bronze reused from other objects. Harald inherited the scale from his father, who was also a baker. Most of the locals in and around Hedeby tend not to use coins when they buy bread from Harald. Instead, they barter. One of Harald's neighbours, for example, brings eggs in return for a loaf of bread, while another from the outskirts of the town brings fresh milk. In this way, Harald gets honey, fish and many other commodities without the exchange of money.

The rooster crows. Harald turns onto his side to look at Sigrid, his beautiful wife, lying next to him. He knows she is not at all a morning person, so he gives her a couple more minutes to enjoy her sleep before he gently elbows her. She rolls over onto her stomach, pulling the bed sheet over her head. He nudges her again, this time a little more firmly. It is the same every morning.

'Is it already time to get up?' she asks with a big yawn.

'Yes,' he says. 'We need to get our bread ready.'

He looks at her long, tousled hair, and for a split second he

A RANGE OF COINS THAT WOULD HAVE BEEN USED IN THE VIKING AGE –
THE SECOND ROW SHOWS THE REVERSE SIDES OF THE COINS.

feels tempted to stay in bed with her and ignore his business. But Harald and Sigrid soon get up, put on their clothes and check on their two young children, who sleep in the same room as them behind a partition wall, and see that they are fast asleep. She and Harald always let them sleep longer, knowing that they need their sleep in order to grow. The children still have plenty of chores during the day, including fetching water, hauling in bags of flour, dragging in firewood and helping their mother wash clothes in the brook. Soon enough they will be called upon to help with the family business.

By Hedeby standards, Harald's house is quite large. It is timber-framed with wattle-and-daub in-filling. The roof is thatched with straw and reeds, with a hole above the hearth in the middle of the house to allow the smoke to escape. In addition, they have an outbuilding used for breadmaking. Their rectangular, fenced-in plot, however, is small, and there are times when Harald envies his farmer friends who do not live so close to their neighbours. Although he is grateful for the rooster, he sometimes gets annoyed when he has to listen to his neighbours' babies crying or when he has no choice but to overhear arguments between a husband and wife.

Their house has three rooms: a living room in the middle and two smaller rooms at either end. One of the smaller rooms is their bedroom, the other their storage room. Their daily life orbits around the fire on a slightly raised, stone-lined hearth in the middle of the floor in their living room. In the centre of the outbuilding is the main source of their livelihood: a large bread oven made on a framework of wattle and shaped like a dome. The outbuilding also stores a fold-out table, which

A RECONSTRUCTION OF A VIKING AGE BREAD OVEN, THIS ONE LOCATED
AT THE VIKINGECENTER IN DENMARK.

Harald sets up outside his house every morning in order to sell his goods.

Most of his craftsman friends and neighbours carry their goods to the large open-air market in Hedeby, where they display their wares on stalls or laid out on the ground, but Harald does not want to bring his warm bread to the market. Besides, he needs to be at home to keep baking until mid-morning, when business finally slows down. Because Harald is the only baker in town, selling out of his home has never been a problem. If the aroma from his bakery does not guide the sailors and traders to his house of business, he knows that word-of-mouth will – and that they will welcome their short walk from the harbour to his house after spending weeks on a cramped ship.

Sigrid starts the day by bringing in water. Like most other people in Hedeby, she and Harald have their own well, which is situated behind their house. It is not particularly deep, but so far they have never experienced a shortage of water. Their well is box-shaped and built of boards around four corner posts. Other wells in the community include circular wells built of barrel staves or hollowed-out tree trunks.

Meanwhile, Harald begins his day with a short visit to his neighbours. He does not have far to go and does not have to worry about vehicular traffic. The two streets in Hedeby, both made of planks, are narrow. The boards are fastened with wooden rivets to parallel rods that run the length of each street. His immediate neighbours are craftsmen – a shoemaker, a metalworker and an artisan who produces glass and amber beads – and, like him, they tend to get up early. The shoemaker does not make much money from visitors and relies mostly on business from locals. But the metalworker and the artisan, like Harald, depend on the trading ships to sell their goods, so he typically meets with them first thing in the morning to find out the latest news on the ship arrivals.

Harald knocks on the shoemaker's door, but no one opens it, so he guesses his friend probably decided to sleep in. He then goes to the metalworker's house and finds him talking with the glass and amber artisan. The two have already been to the harbour to check on the two ships. The metalworker reports that one ship, which he thinks came from Norway, is carrying vessels and bowls made of soapstone, as well as iron bars that are probably for export to places farther away. The artisan believes that the other ship came from the Baltic, carrying salt and spices, wine and silks for import. At the harbour, they also found the ships' many crew members asleep on the shore, because Hedeby is renowned for being safe from pirates, so they don't need to stay on board to protect their stock-in-trade.

When Harald returns to his house, he quickly feeds the fire under their oven, as he has spent too much time chatting with the neighbours. He finds Sigrid busy kneading dough on the table in the outbuilding. As usual, Harald had laid out the varieties of flour on the table last evening to make things easier and faster for today. He wraps his hands around Sigrid's waist, which startles her for a second. She does not mind, though. She turns around, giving him a big smile. 'It's going to be a good day,' she says and kisses him on the cheek.

Harald buys his flour from local farmers, who have already ground it for him in hand querns. The farmers deliver it to his house once a week, so all he and his children have to do is haul in the flour, which they keep in the storage room of their house. Harald and Sigrid make a variety of breads, buns and cakes, using several types of flour, though barley is a main ingredient in most of their baked goods. When they run low on barley, they can extend it by mixing other grains, such as linseed, pea flour or pine bark.

Barley cake is one of their most popular sellers because it is inexpensive, so Sigrid decides to start with that. Besides, the preparation of barley dough is easy. All she has to do is mix the barley flour with water or milk and add a little salt and honey. She shapes the dough into small balls, squishes them flat and puts them in the oven. This time, however, she has overestimated the amount of dough needed for her cake. She is not one to let anything go to waste, so she adds lard and some flax seeds to the leftover dough and kneads it again. It's not often that she can be creative, and she quickly forms four small round breads from the dough. She makes four pinch marks around the tops of each loaf, then assembles them into a single cake in the shape of a four-leaf clover. Once the barley cakes come out of the oven, this more unusual creation goes in.

Meanwhile, Harald starts making rye bread, which is another favourite, especially among locals. He shapes the dough into fairly large round balls, then flattens them a bit. Baking rye bread takes longer and there are limits to how much bread can be baked in the oven at one time, so Harald puts the rye bread in the oven as soon as possible. Meanwhile, Sigrid is in a hurry. Because of their slightly late start this morning, she is worried they may not have enough bread for their early-morning customers. She runs now to put the barley cakes on the table outside and then starts the fire in the living room, where she will bake the flat bread in a suspended pan. Once prepared, flat bread does not take long to bake. The basic ingredients are wheat flour and water or milk. To add flavouring, she just uses whatever is in season, such as seeds from the beech tree, broadleaf plaintain, hacked nuts or finely hacked fruit. It is early in the summer, so she does not yet have blueberries, raspberries or apples and resorts to using a little bit of honey and some hazelnuts stored from the year before. She glances at her husband and can see that he has now almost finished making oat bread, which will go into the oven as soon as the rye bread comes out. Sometimes, Harald makes sourdough loaves, but not today. In order to make sourdough, he needs old bread, but he has none now because sales over the past few days were so good they totally sold out. On rare occasions, he makes bread using wheat, but only on demand. This so-called 'white bread' is very expensive, and only the wealthiest of customers can afford it.

The barley cakes, rye bread, flat bread and four-leaf clover loaf are now on display on the table in front of the house, and the oat bread is almost ready to come out of the oven. Harald grabs his money box and the scale with its weights, and sees a man walking up the narrow street towards his house with a bag in his hand. The man looks carefully at all the baked goods with pleasure on his face. Harald does not recognize him. From his unkempt appearance, Harald thinks he must be a sailor, and maybe one of those who decided to sleep on the beach. The man first points to the four-leaf clover bread and then to the flat bread, signing with his fingers that he wants three of those. Then he points to the rye breads signing with his fingers that he wants one of those. He pays in good silver and Harald can see him take a huge bite from the four-leaf clover bread as he walks off.

Harald would never know that Hedeby would be destroyed by fire around 1050 and again in 1066, possibly by King Harald Hardruler of Norway or by the Wends. This was the end of Hedeby's life as a trading centre. After that, the town was permanently abandoned. In its place, Schleswig, only a few miles away, was founded as its successor.

11TH HOUR OF THE NIGHT
(04.00–05.00)

A TRADER GATHERS
HIS GOODS

Ottar is walking towards his ship, which he keeps in a sheltered area by the bay. He has been on his feet for hours; at his home in Hålogaland in northern Norway, the sun hardly sets in the summer, so it feels like he is busy all the time. He considers himself a famer, although grain farming is almost impossible because of the rugged terrain, the short summers and the cool weather. His farm livestock consists of twenty sheep, twenty swine and a couple of horses, which he uses to plough what little good ground there is to plough. He feeds his animals mostly on the hay his wife and children can rake together in the summer and store in their barn. He also owns 600 tame reindeer, of which six are decoys that he uses for catching wild reindeer.

He and his family can live quite cheaply this far north. The reindeer cost nothing to raise beyond the labour of their capture, and they do not have to be fed. In the summer, the reindeer find their own food among mosses, herbs, ferns, grasses and the shoots and leaves of shrubs and trees. In the winter, they live off the lichen they uncover by scraping away the hard snow with their hooves. Although it is possible for Ottar to sustain himself and his family on what he earns from his land and animals, he wants a better lifestyle and more commodities than the farm can provide. Over the years, he has amassed quite a bit of wealth through other means, including from taxes paid by the Sámi people.

Ottar does not fully understand the history of this tax and its true purpose, but he believes it was started as a tribute paid by the Sámi in exchange for protection. Their tax consists of the pelts of wild beasts, the feathery down of birds, whalebone and ship cables made from the skins of whales and seals. Each Sámi man pays an annual tax according to his rank in society. The higher his status, the more he must pay. For example, the highest-born must pay fifteen marten skins, five reindeer skins, one bear skin, ten bushels of down, a short coat of bear or otter skin and two cables, each sixty ells long, one whale-hide and one of seal. Hunting is another lucrative source of income for Ottar. Northern Norway is known for its great whale- and walrus-hunting, especially walrus. Once, Ottar and five of his men managed to kill no fewer than sixty walruses in just two days.

During the past couple of weeks, Ottar and his men have been busy inspecting his ship and smearing it with seal oil in

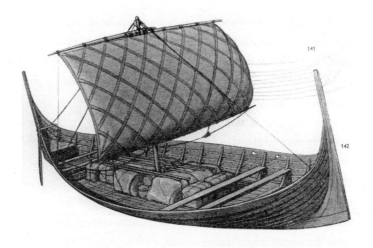

A DRAWING OF A VIKING CARGO SHIP, SHOWING ITS SQUARE SAIL AND RAISED BOW, AND THE CARGO COMPARTMENT BELOW DECK.

preparation for their upcoming journey. Ottar's ship is a cross between a travel ship and a cargo ship. Made of pine and ash, it has an open cargo hold amidship, with a permanent deck and oar holes fore and aft, and a firmly placed mast designed to be lowered when needed. Ottar relies almost exclusively on the sails for propulsion when at sea. He uses the oars only when the ship is becalmed or when it must be manoeuvred near landing places. It is a convenient ship, requiring only a small crew – a helmsman, one or two men to bail seawater and a few others to handle the sail. Because the ship is so comfortable, Ottar and his men don't mind spending their days and nights at sea, but the coastline along western Norway where they are heading this time is very long. For this trip, he has decided to bring a small boat which will be towed astern, so he and his crew can row ashore whenever they want to cook and sleep in tents for a break, or when they need to replenish their water and food supplies along the way.

Ottar is very satisfied with his ship. It serves him well, especially during the summers when he travels south to sell his goods. One summer, however, he abandoned his usual travel plans and decided to explore the lands to the north. He wanted to see how much futher north the land stretched and if the walrus-hunting might be better there. For the first three days, he sailed along the coast and saw nothing but wasteland to starboard and open sea to port. He sensed then that he must be as far north as any hunters would ever have gone for whales, but he was still curious to see what might lie beyond. Ottar ordered his helmsman to continue on for yet another three days, when he noticed that the land seemed to him to curve eastward. There, he had to pause and wait for a west-north-west wind so he could sail on. And sail on he did, along the coast for four more days, when again he noticed another shift in the curve of the land, this time to the south. To continue on, he had to wait there for the right kind of wind, this time from the north. When it came, he sailed due south along the coast as far as he could reach in five days, when to starboard he could see that a mighty river had carved an opening into the land and now poured its fresh water into the sea. Ottar was tempted to sail beyond this river but decided against it, for he could see that the land was continuously settled on the far bank of the river, and he knew that he and his men had no secure right of passage beyond this point. Up until now, he had not come upon any cultivated land since he had left his home. The only people he had seen were nomadic fishermen, fowlers and hunters – all of them Sámi. So, he decided to end his voyage of exploration right there and returned home.

Now, Ottar arrives at his ship and sees that his men have finished loading it with the wares he hopes to sell in the south – furs and feathers and ropes of walrus and seal hide, as well as walrus ivory, a very sought-after commodity used in decorative art abroad. Ottar briefly considers also bringing along some seal blubber as well but changes his mind because he and his family may need the oil from the blubber for their lamps during the upcoming long, dark winter.

From Scandinavia, mainly fish, metals and to some degree butter and meat entered long-distance trade. Stockfish from northern Norway was the first Scandinavian-produced commodity sold in large quantities on North European markets.

While Ottar waits for his wife and children to arrive with food, water and extra clothing for his voyage, he carefully explains the route he wants to take to his helmsman and the small crew. It is not as if they do not know the route, because they have taken it several times before, but this is the first time Ottar's eldest son, Olaf, a teenager, is coming along. His job is to bail seawater during the trip.

'First, we sail along the coast of Norway to Kaupang in southern Norway,' he says. He warns them that even if they have a favourable wind, it could be a long voyage, up to a month if they have to anchor at night. He says that sometimes the sea can be rough, even though they will be sailing close to land. During the trip, they will likely stay in Kaupang for a few days, he says. Then, mostly for the sake of Olaf, he explains that Kaupang is one of the main outlets of trade for Vestfold, and that they will meet other northern merchants there with cargoes of furs, skins, down, walrus ivory, hide ropes, soapstone and iron. 'From Kaupang,' he continues, 'we will sail further south, with Denmark to port and open sea to starboard, and then, with Jutland and the cluster of Danish islands to starboard. We will sail until we reach Hedeby, our ultimate destination.'

From experience, he estimates that this last leg of the voyage to Hedeby should only take about five days, if the winds are on their side, and that he plans to stay in Hedeby for roughly a week. After that, they will return to Hålogaland with their goods, sailing back the same way they came. He hopes they won't have to anchor at night very often, because for Ottar and other merchants living so far north, the sailing season is short and he wants to avoid severe autumn storms.

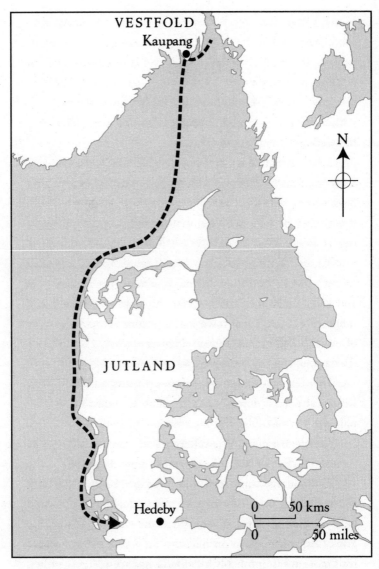

A MAP DEPICTING OTTAR AND HIS CREW'S ROUTE TO HEDEBY.

Although Ottar has tried to prime Olaf for this trip by taking him sailing several times, he can see from the expression on his son's face that he is nervous. After all, Olaf has never been away from his mother and siblings for more than a couple of days. Ottar assures his son that while the first stretch of the voyage may be long and potentially rough, sailing in Danish waters will be easy.

'You just have to hang in there. I know you're not going to get seasick,' he says to Olaf. 'You're a grown man now, and you'll make me proud.' Ottar thinks his son will find it interesting to see a real town and tells him Hedeby has a lot of exciting things to offer, especially tasty and exotic foods, and that he will enjoy the warmer temperatures. To cheer him up, Ottar tells him that in Hedeby he plans to buy salt, spices, wine and pottery for the general household in Hålogaland, plus weapons for Olaf and his brothers, semi-precious stones for his sisters, a piece of jewellery for his mother and maybe even some cloth of silk, if he can make a good bargain.

'And you, my son,' he says, 'will pick out something that you really like in return for your help. Maybe you can even help me choose a fine silver brooch for your mother.' Ottar gives Olaf a firm clasp on his shoulder and can tell he now feels more at ease, probably because he has been called a grown man and there is a good prospect of a present or two for him.

Ottar turns around and sees his wife and their children approaching with the food, drinks and clothing he ordered for the trip. Even his little children are helping to carry the many things. Ottar does not like being away from the home for so long every summer and feels some guilt that his wife and their other older children now have to be in charge of everything on the farm. He knows she has a lot on her plate, not only making food and looking after the younger children but also supervising the older children to make sure they do their chores around the farm, including feeding the domestic animals, raking hay, doing laundry in the brook and gathering berries. He and his wife have often talked about her heavier workload, especially now she will lose the services of Olaf, their oldest. In fact, they spoke about it again last evening. Ottar tried to have a serious conversation with her, but she just joked, saying it might be fun to get pregnant in the autumn and give birth to a baby in the summer. She was adamant that he continue his work as a trader as she really appreciates the goods he brings home, especially the salt and the spices, which enable her to make their food more tasty. 'But don't forget', she said, 'to bring nice gifts home for the children and a piece of jewellery for me.'

Olaf relieves his mother and siblings of the supplies they are carrying, brings them on board the ship and then goes back to join his family to say his farewell. The rest of the crew are already on board, eagerly waiting to depart. Ottar hugs his children, especially the little ones. He worries they will have forgotten him by the time he returns. He recalls coming home in the early autumn only to find his young children fearing him. They did not recognize him as their father.

Finally, he gives his wife a long and touching embrace. 'Be brave,' he says to her, and she nods. He can tell she is trying hard to hide her emotions, that she does not want him to see she is on the verge of tears. After a final squeeze and a kiss, he lets go of her and boards his ship. With a favourable wind, his men cheerfully lift the anchor, raise the sail and are off. Ottar watches his family climb a cliff to watch them sail away for as long as they can. They wave and wave to him and Olaf, who wave back until they are finally out of sight.

Ottar would never know that the account of his travels, which years later he would narrate to Alfred, king of the Anglo-Saxon kingdom of Wessex, would one day be incorporated into an Old English adaptation of a Latin historical book, *Seven Books of History Against the Pagans*, written early in the fifth century by Paulus Orosius.

12TH HOUR OF THE NIGHT
(05.00–06.00)

A WOMAN DEFENDS
HER PEOPLE

Freydis, daughter of Eirik the Red, wakes up early in the morning to great commotion outside the group of houses she and other Norse Greenlanders have built in North America. They call their new home Hop. A year ago, she and her husband, Thorvard of Gardar, were members of the mighty Greenland expedition led here by Thorfin Karlsefni, a wealthy and distinguished sea-going merchant, and his friend Snorri Thorbrandsson.

It was during the winter before, while they were still back in their Norse settlement at Brattahlid, just east of the southern tip of Greenland, that there had been much discussion about heading west to settle the new land which Freydis' brother,

Leif Eiriksson, had explored a few years earlier. Leif had learned about the land from a merchant, Bjarni Herjolfsson, who had discovered it by accident. Leif listened intently as Bjarni told him the tale of his trip:

'I'd come to Iceland from Norway in the summer, only to find out my father and Eirik the Red had recently emigrated from Iceland to Greenland. So, I decided to sail from Iceland to Greenland with my cargo, thinking the new Greenland settlers needed my goods more than the Icelanders. But on my way to Greenland, I was met with fog and unfavourable winds, and I didn't know my whereabouts. That's when I saw some land which I knew was not Greenland, but I didn't want to take the time to explore it then because autumn was drawing on. I had to get my cargo to Greenland as quickly as possible, so I left.'

Leif was so curious about this new land that he bought Bjarni's ship, sailed the merchant's course in reverse, and found it. Leif and his men stayed there for part of the summer and even built some houses. When Leif returned to Greenland, he raved about the country he had named Vinland. 'There's good land to be had there,' he said, 'with fields of wild wheat, lush vines and forests of maple trees.'

Intrigued by Leif's description, Thorfin decided to settle in Vinland and invited others to join him. It was not an easy decision for Freydis, her husband or the others to leave their homes, but many had found life to be too harsh in Greenland, where the winters were so long and frigid and where animal husbandry and grain farming were so difficult. Eventually, Freydis and Thorvard made up their minds to relocate to

North America in search of a better life. Many others soon agreed. Thorfin and Snorri sailed off with three ships and no fewer than 160 men and women.

But now, Freydis is annoyed at having been awakened so early. Because she is heavily pregnant, she does not sleep well these days, and last night it was late before she finally got comfortable. She impatiently steps outside the house, scantily clothed and without shoes, to see what is going on. She is startled to find a fierce battle raging between her compatriots and the people known as the Skraelings. It is easy to tell them apart, for the Skraelings are shorter in stature, with tangled hair, large eyes and broad cheekbones.

Skraeling is the name the Norse Greenlanders used for the indigenous people they encountered in North America. Both the meaning and the etymology of the word have been debated among scholars. So far, there is no consensus. The term is used in Old Norse-Icelandic literature about both the Inuit and native Americans.

Freydis has seen these Skraelings before. A few weeks ago, the Norse Greenlanders had caught sight of nine skin boats early one morning. The men in the boats were waving their sticks at them sunwise, from left to right, like the course the sun takes across the sky. Thorfin, Snorri and their men took this as a sign of peace, so they took their white shields and went to meet their visitors, who then rowed their boats ashore. The two groups of men stared and marvelled at each other before the visitors rowed away towards the south, around the headland and out of sight.

A couple of weeks later the Skraelings came back, but this time they came in much greater numbers, with so many boats someone said the estuary appeared to be strewn with charcoal. Their sticks were again waved sunwise, so Thorfin Karlsefni and his men raised their white shields in return. The Skraelings spoke words the settlers did not understand, but from their hand gestures it became apparent they wished to trade. At first, they wanted swords and spears, which Thorfin and Snorri forbade. The Skraelings then indicated that they wanted to trade their grey pelts for the settlers' red cloth. For each of their pelts, the Skraelings received a span of cloth, about nine inches long, which they tied around their heads. The trading went on this way until the cloth was beginning to run out, so Thorfin and his men decided to cut their cloth into narrower strips, no more than a finger's breadth wide, while still charging the same amount and sometimes even more. The trading went on again until a huge bull, which Thorfin Karlsefni and his men had brought from Greenland, charged suddenly out of the woods, bellowing furiously. The

Skraelings ran to their boats in terror and rowed off, with their red headbands tossing in the wind.

Freydis now seeks solace with a woman standing outside the house. She tells Freydis that earlier that morning the men saw a huge number of boats, pouring in 'like a torrent', only this time the Skraelings were waving their sticks anti-sunwise and howling loudly. So, she says, the men had hoisted their red shields and advanced towards the Skraelings. 'Not good,' the woman says. 'I think we're in deep trouble.'

Freydis watches as a hail of missiles flies over the defenders, so she quickly steps back inside the house. When she comes out again, she sees the attackers now hoisting a large round object onto a dark blue pole, which they use to hurl the object at Thorfin Karlsefni's men. It makes a loud crash when it strikes the ground. The Norse Greenlanders startle at this and begin to flee to safety further up the river. They run until they reach some cliffs, where they eventually decide to make their stand against the Skraelings.

Freydis is horrified and angered at the defenders' lack of courage and yells out, 'Why do you flee from such pitiful wretches, brave men like you? You should be able to slaughter them like cattle. If I had weapons, I'm sure I could fight better than any of you!' But none of them pay her any heed, not even her husband. Even though her ankles are swollen and the weight of the baby inside her makes it hard for her to move, she is now so annoyed with them she decides to join them at the cliffs. By the time she gets there, the men have run away again, this time retreating into the woods. Freydis can hear women calling her to return to the house, but she ignores them, even though she notices that the Skraelings have begun to close in on her.

It is then that she sees a dead man lying in front of her. She recognizes him as Thorbrand Snorrason, a member of the expedition. He has a flint stone buried in his head. His sword lies next to him. In panic, Freydis grabs his sword off the ground and prepares to defend herself and her unborn child, but she is not sure how to handle the weapon, never having wielded a sword before. When the Skraelings finally rush towards her, all she can think of is to pull one of her breasts out of her bodice. She slaps it with the hilt of the sword to show that she is a woman and not afraid to fight. The Skraelings freeze, then cautiously form a circle around her and stare at her in amazement. They begin to speak quietly to each other, then suddenly flee in panic back to their boats and hasten away.

Now that it is safe, Thorfin and his men run to her. Thorvard hugs her tightly and then strokes her belly. 'I hope the baby is alright,' he says.

Freydis looks at him in disbelief and thinks to herself: 'How could you be more concerned about the baby than me?'

Thorfin Karlsefni thanks her and praises her for her courage. He reports that four Skraelings have been killed compared with only two of their men, though they had been fighting against heavy odds. 'You made us proud,' Thorfin says. 'I can't believe your courage. You saved many men's lives, maybe the lives of all of us.'

The men lead Freydis back to the houses and encourage her to sit and rest on the grass, when she realizes that she still has Thorbrand's sword in her hand. 'Just as well,' she thinks to herself. 'I might need it again.' It is only then she realizes that her breast is still uncovered, and though it hurts a bit from the impact of the sword, she quickly tucks it back into her bodice, flushing with embarrassment. She cannot believe that her husband did not tell her on their way back from the woods. Some of the women bring her water, food and a blanket to lie down on. One woman combs Freydis' long, dishevelled hair, then takes her hand. 'You need to rest and calm down,' she says. 'We don't want you to give birth until the baby is ready.'

Thorfin calls together all the Norse settlers for a meeting on the grass where Freydis is lying. It is clear to her that everyone is as shaken as she is about what happened. Thorfin Karlsefni and Snorri talk very quietly together, but eventually Thorfin raises his voice and says to the crowd: 'I want to talk to you very seriously about this venture. I think it was a mistake, and I don't think it's feasible for us to settle here. What we've found is not Leif's Vinland, and we're clearly unable to defend ourselves against the Skraelings. There are many of them and few of us. I recommend that we return to Greenland.'

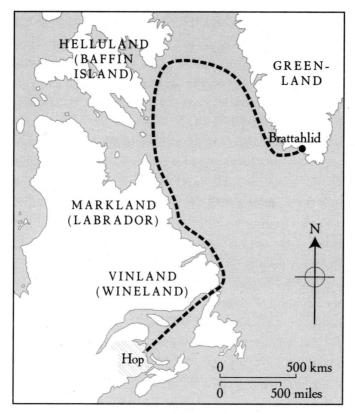

A MAP SHOWING FREYDIS' JOURNEY FROM GREENLAND TO HOP.

Freydis does not know what to think. She remembers the long voyage from Greenland to Hop, during which she had been seasick almost all the time. First, they had sailed from Brattahlid, the so-called Eastern Settlement in Greenland, to the so-called Western Settlement further north of the west coast of Greenland. Then they sailed before a northerly wind, and after two days at sea they finally sighted land. Some of the men rowed ashore to explore, using the boats they had towed. They reported back that there were many foxes there, and that they had found many slabs of stone, so huge that two men could stretch out on them sole to sole.

That was clearly not Leif's Vinland, and so they sailed for two more days before a northerly wind. When they sighted land ahead again, some of the men rowed ashore and reported back that it was heavily wooded and abounding with animals. Freydis would have liked to settle there, but the men decided to continue in search of Leif's Vinland, and after another two days of sailing, they sighted land again and sailed towards it before they realized they were approaching a promontory. They tacked along the coast with the land to starboard.

The coastline was open and harbourless with long beaches and extensive sands everywhere. It seemed to take forever to sail past it until, finally, the land became indented with bays. They steered into one of them and came to a river that flowed down into a lake and from the lake into the sea. There were many long sandbars outside the river mouth, so their ships could only enter it at high tide. Karlsefni and his company sailed into the lagoon and called the land Hop. Much to Freydis' relief, they cast anchor and decided to settle there.

Freydis prefers life at Hop in North America to life at Brattahlid in Greenland. Here, just as Leif had said, there is wild wheat growing in fields on all the low ground and grape vines on all the hills. Every stream is teeming with fish. When they first arrived, the men dug trenches at the high-tide mark, and when the tide went out there were halibut trapped in the trenches. In the woods, there are a great number of animals of all kinds. And in the winter, there is hardly any snow. The thought of returning to Greenland and giving birth on a ship does not appeal to her – but she knows she has no say in this. Only her husband, Thorvard, can protest, but he looks away when she tries to make eye contact with him. She is not surprised. She knows that he is more of a follower than a leader, and there have been times when she wished she had married someone with more backbone. No one says anything. 'Alright then,' Thorfin Karlsefni says. 'Since no one objects to my recommendation, we'll now start packing our things and prepare the ships for the return voyage. The sailing season is short, and we need to get back to Greenland before the autumn.'

Freydis goes back into her house. Sadly, she begins to gather her few belongings. She knows there is no way she and Thorvald can stay behind in Hop by themselves. She must leave her new home in North America. She looks around, admires the vegetation and the beautiful streams, and sighs.

Leif named the lands as he and his crew sailed along the eastern shore of North America. He called the first Helluland ('flat-stone land') – maybe Baffin Island. He called the second Markland ('forest land') – maybe Labrador. It was the third that he called Vinland ('wine land'), which has not yet been located with any certainty. Most likely, Vinland is not a specific site but a region which included Newfoundland and extended south into the Gulf of St Lawrence as far as Nova Scotia. Evidence that the Norsemen came to North America is evident from the L'Anse aux Meadows archaeological site, first excavated in the 1960s.

Freydis would never know that it would be about 500 years before another white man – Christopher Columbus – would be back to 'discover' North America, again.

1ST HOUR OF THE DAY
(06.00–07.00)

A BABY IS SPARED
FROM BEING EXPOSED

Grim Thorgeirsson (Signyarson) is standing in front of his farmhouse at Grimsstadir, surveying his property and thinking about the work that needs to be done around the farm. He directs his farmhands to start repairing some of the stone fences. He is proud of his farm. His farmhouse is more luxurious than many others in Iceland with its partition walls dividing the interior into rooms which can be closed off. He has also added four outbuildings over recent years – a bathhouse, a barn for animal fodder, a stable and his latest and proudest addition: a byre for wintering the domestic animals. For years, these animals had roomed at the end of the longhouse during the winter, but Grim had become tired of living with them.

Although the animals' body heat helped keep the cold away, the flies and flees they attracted annoyed him and his wife Helga.

The longhouse is now used solely as a family and household living space and for cooking. Helga, a good homemaker, has done much to make the longhouse more pleasant and inviting. The woollen blankets she has woven grace the raised platforms along the walls of the house. She has made tapestries too, which now decorate and help insulate the walls. Grim is contented and considers himself well married.

He goes inside to have breakfast with Helga, the farmhands and the servant women. While eating, they hear a knock on the door. Grim is surprised to have visitors so early in the morning but rises to greet them. He recognizes Sigmund and his wife and son, a family of beggars who have visited several times before. In fact, Grim has often invited them to stay for days when the weather was inclement, because he enjoys their company. Sigmund is a good storyteller and provides welcome news and gossip about what he has seen and heard on his roamings around the country, while Sigmund's wife is helpful around the house and their son, a young teenager, is well behaved. This time, Sigmund also cradles a baby in his arm. Grim is not particularly surprised, because he has heard rumours from neighbours that the family has been travelling with a baby in tow. Many have questioned, though, if it is truly Sigmund's child.

The family is clearly tired and no doubt hungry, so Grim invites them in and offers them a seat on the raised platforms. Helga quickly feeds the long fire, thinking they may be cold after walking all night, and offers them breakfast: a hearty meal of porridge and flatbread. When they have finished, Grim asks to see the baby, but Sigmund seems very reluctant. He tells Grim that it is too much trouble to loosen the baby's bindings and that it would be difficult to comfort her, warning that she would likely cry a lot and for a long time. But Grim insists.

Like his neighbours, Grim has suspicions about the baby and can tell by the look in Helga's eyes that she, too, wants to see it. Sigmund realizes he has no choice, asks his wife to unbind the child and reveals the baby to Grim. One look and Grim knows that the baby is his half-sister: his mother, Signy Valbrandsdottir, had given birth to a girl only months earlier and died in childbirth. Signy's second husband and the girl's father, Grimkel Bjarnarson, had not been there for the birth. The parents-to-be had not been getting along, so Signy received permission from Grimkel to take a holiday at Breidabolstad, owned by her brother and Grim's uncle, Torfi Valbrandsson, even though Grimkel and Torfi detested each other. Grimkel never came to see his wife or their new baby girl.

Grim recognizes the baby not only from her beautiful eyes, inherited from their mother, but also because he and Helga had cared for the baby for a brief time shortly after her birth. A couple of months ago, Grim, who always goes outside before breakfast to decide on the tasks of the day, had noticed a man sprint towards his farm, place something in one of his gateways and then race off again. Because the morning was overcast and the sun only starting to rise, Grim was not positive, but he thought the man to be Sigurd Gunnhildarson, Torfi's foster son.

'What could he possibly have dropped off,' Grim had wondered. When he checked, he was astonished to find an infant girl, only hours old, wrapped in a tiny blanket. He was unsure what to do. He and Helga had no children and certainly no experience with newborns. But his instincts told him to pick up the baby, and he found her healthy and beautiful – not at all the type of infant that, according to Icelandic law, could be exposed due to deformity or illness. Grim brought the baby inside to Helga, explained the situation and then quickly sprinkled her with water, naming her Thorbjörg after his favourite god.

Children were considered to belong to the male parent, as revealed by the nomenclature that identified a person as the son or daugther of a man by affixing -son or -dottir to his or her name. The naming was often accompanied by the sprinkling of water. The importance of sprinkling is suggested by the declaration in the laws that 'it was called murder when children were killed after water had been poured over them'.

He and Helga soon came up with a plan: she would pretend to go into labour, lie down in bed and say to anyone who might ask that she had just given birth to this little girl. She assured Grim that one of the servant women could nurse the baby. When Grim saw Helga in bed with Thorbjörg, it was clear just how happy his wife was to have the infant in her arms.

After Helga and the baby were settled, Grim set out for Breidabolstad, hoping to find out who had left the child at his farm and why. But as he approached the farm, he saw a large number of people walking out of the yard and found out that the gathering was his mother's funeral procession. Though in shock, he joined in and attended the funeral. After that, he talked with Torfi, who had had little to say, except that from then on he would have nothing more to do with his mother's widower Grimkel. Any future dealings with Signy's husband would be Grim's responsibility.

Eventually, Grim also tracked down Sigurd, who confessed that Torfi had refused to have the baby sprinkled and named and had told him to drown the baby in the Reykjadalsa river. Sigurd had tried to resist Torfi, telling him it was an evil thing to do because the baby was healthy, but he dared not refuse the order because he feared retaliations from hot-tempered Torfi. He feared for his life. So he had gone to the river, but once there he simply could not throw the baby into the water. She looked too beautiful and promising. He soon found himself walking towards Grimsstadir, and in desperation he placed the baby in Grim's gateway in the hope it would be found. Grim took pity on the young man. Together, they walked back to Grimsstadir, where Grim gave Sigurd two horses, one to ride and one to carry his packed provisions. From there, he sent him south to Eyrar, to board a ship out of the country and safely away from Torfi.

Before the conversion to Christianity, child abandonment was a commonly accepted social tradition. The unwanted infant was wrapped in cloth and left in the wilderness to be exposed to the elements. Infanticide was most often inflicted on baby girls.

The next day, Torfi walked to Grimsstadir to find out if anyone knew the whereabouts of Sigurd. According to Helga, Torfi walked right in without knocking and expressed surprise to find her in bed. She calmly told Torfi that she had given birth, but when he saw the baby next to her he became very angry. 'How dare you and Grim raise the child I'd ordered exposed,' he said, then stormed outside looking for Grim, who was with his farmhands. He berated Grim, then asked him if he knew where Sigurd might be. Grim told him the truth: he had sent Sigurd to the fjords to board a ship. Torfi flew into a rage, stormed back into the house, snatched the baby from Helga and returned to his farm. Grim and Helga were devastated, but they were consoled by the fact that Torfi could not have the baby killed now. If he did kill the baby, it would be murder under the law, for the child had been sprinkled with water and named. Later, Grim heard from neighbours that Torfi had soon tired of having the baby around and had given her to one of his slave women. But that was not the end of Thorbjörg's story.

Grim now glances at Helga, who looks so happy holding the baby again. Grim wonders how and why Sigmund, a vagrant, ended up with Thorbjörg, carrying her from farm to farm. Sigmund relates that he had come to Breidabolstad asking for lodging. Torfi had said his family could stay in the guest house for a day or two, but that in return for the hospitality he must take the little girl to Ölfusvatn, to her biological father, Grimkel. Sigmund was hesitant but eventually agreed, as he had no choice. The new family of four took off for Ölfusvatn, but progress was slow, Sigmund explains. Wherever they stayed along the way, the people saw they were carrying a baby and kindly invited them to stay longer, and it was difficult not to accept their hospitality. For that reason, he says, they took the longest route possible because they could rely on lodging and food. Eventually, they arrived at Ölfusvatn , where Sigmund found Grimkel sitting on his bed in his house with a sword across his knees.

'Introduce yourself,' Grimkel said.

'I'm Sigmund, the foster father of your daughter Thorbjörg,' Sigmund replied.

Grimkel, quickly enraged, said, 'I cannot believe that you, a tramp, can be the foster father of my child!' He lashed out at Torfi. 'How could he hate me so? First he kills my wife and then he drives my child into beggary from house to house just to humiliate me.' He threatened Sigmund with beatings or worse unless he left immediately. 'And take the baby with you!' he shouted.

That was the last they saw of Grimkel. For the past few weeks, he and his family had wandered the country around Grimsnes and Laurgardale and eventually run out of good places to stay. He tells Grim that he finally realized they had nowhere else to go but Grimsstadir.

Grim takes a while to absorb all this new information. He glances at Helga, who is holding Thorbjörg and seems as happy as he has ever seen her. Though her bindings have been removed, the baby does not fuss or cry, contented in the warmth of Helga's body and a blanket loosely wrapped around her. Eventually, Grim makes eye contact with Helga and she quietly nods. She knows what he is thinking and silently agrees with him.

'I'll take the child and care for her and relieve you of your duties,' he says to Sigmund. 'Thank you for bringing her to us.'

Grim invites the travellers to stay for a few days. He looks once again at Helga, who is smiling, with a sparkle in her eyes he has never seen before. He knows he has made the right decision and smiles back at her.

A MAN PREPARES FOR MILITARY ACTION

Hans Jensson is waiting outside the door of his farmhouse near the small town of Ribe on the west coast of Jutland. He is anxious, waiting for the rest of the crew members to arrive, but the dense fog limits his vision to barely twenty feet. He walks closer to the edge of his property to see if the view is any clearer from there, but no, the fog keeps rolling in. Hans grew up here and has learned to live with the fog, but today he wishes it would go away.

Hans owns his farm. Recently, he and other free farmers along the coasts of Denmark were commissioned by King Cnut the Great to organize coastal fleets. The purpose: to help with seasonal excursions and to defend the realm. His commission is supposed to be an honour, he knows that, but Hans realizes it comes with much responsibility and sacrifice for him, his family and his crew members.

Denmark has been divided into several ship-providing districts through a so-called levy system. The monarch serves as its chief military leader, while the free farmers in each district are to provide ships of forty, forty-two or fifty oars. They must also recruit the men for their ships' crews, including enough equipment and supplies for them to be at sea for up to three months. Each crew member is obliged to provide his own arms – an axe, a spear, a bow with arrows – plus a shield to defend himself.

Although he is not required to be on the ship himself, Hans is also assigned to recruit the steersman, the one to serve as captain of his ship while at sea and to oversee the crew members, the armament and the provisions. When he hears this, Hans immediately calls on his neighbour and good friend Asbjörn Hansson, and asks him to take on the responsibility. He agrees. Though Asbjörn is not a free farmer but a foreman, he skilfully manages the large number of hands on a farm that is doing very well. Hans knows he can trust Asbjörn because he is so reliable. He is also an excellent sailor and will make a terrific chief-in-command at sea.

Hans' time to gather his full crew is running short, and he is getting nervous now as he waits and hopes that the rest of his crew will soon appear through the fog. It was only late yesterday evening, when Hans and his wife Jensina were about to go to bed, that one of King Cnut the Great's envoys came to his farm. The envoy announced that Hans had to assemble his crew for a military action immediately. When Hans asked for more details, the envoy only said his crew must sail north along the coast of Jutland to join other ships gathered there. Then he rushed off on his horse to rally other free farmers to get ready.

Though the envoy's information was vague, Hans doubts this expedition is for defence, as that would require the entire levy to convene. For defence expeditions, all the ships would be told to gather and wait for news about where the enemy is planning to attack. Once the assault location is known, the fleet of fighting units would meet there to engage in battle. They would not be alone. They would be supported by locals, as every man in Denmark is obliged to turn out to fight off invaders. Even the slaves would be allowed to fight, and they have an incentive: if a slave kills an enemy fighter, he will, by law, be granted his freedom.

If an expedition is for offensive purposes, however, only a part of the levy is required to convene, because some forces must remain at home to defend the country if necessary. As Hans stands outside his home now, still waiting for the rest of his crew, he tries to process this information from the king. Since his envoy said nothing about slaves – not that Hans has any – he concludes this must be a request for a seasonal excursion.

Hans was not surprised that Asbjörn dropped everything yesterday evening and came immediately to Hans' farm after learning of the king's call to arms. Nor was he surprised that his enterprising new steersman brought additional weapons and food for the expedition, just in case Hans needed them. The other men that Hans recruited for the crew – relatives and neighbours who readily agreed to serve – are here now, but not all, and he needs them all. This area of Denmark is sparsely populated, so some of his new recruits live a fair distance away, and they might not have received his summons to gather until very early this morning. But he is sure they would have been here by now, if not for the damned fog.

'If only the fog would lift,' he mumbles to himself.

Hans is sure that his ship of forty oars – even though it is a bit old – is sea-worthy and will serve his crew and captain well. It fits in with the other ships in the levy system, as by law the ships must be uniform in construction and equipment so that, when combined, they can easily merge into a fleet that forms a formidable force. He has always taken good care of his ship. He never uses it during the winter months, which would be hard on it, but keeps it in the boathouse his father built close to the shore.

And as luck would have it, he had it serviced only a few

A RECONSTRUCTION OF A VIKING LONGSHIP, SHOWING THE TYPICAL
CONSTRUCTION OF THESE SHIPS. THIS PARTICULAR SHIP IS DOCKED IN
INNERPOLLEN LAKE IN NORWAY.

weeks ago. Not much work was needed. All the strakes that
were fastened with iron nails were secure, though some needed
more caulking with tarred animal hair to ensure the hull would
remain watertight. He also had a nearby boatbuilder make
new oars to replace any that might be showing signs of rot.
That only took a couple of days. He was ready when the order
came down.

But Hans feels uneasy as he faces this, his first time to
take action and oversee an expedition. He begins to question
himself. 'What if I can't live up to the demands?' he wonders.
'How much easier it would be if only it were not so foggy.'
He knows it could be worse, because the sea is at least calm
today, as is typically the case in foggy weather. Hans has
spent enough time on the water to know some things about

the challenges fog can present – the dangers of getting lost or stuck on the many sand reefs in the North Sea along the south coast of Jutland. His own voyages have always been short and limited to easy summer trips to Hedeby, further south, to purchase goods he or Jensina needed, like cloth and spices from abroad. He can only imagine what his missing crew members must be facing now in the chilly spring air, blinded by the fog and racing against time.

Hans remembers the time as a child when he and his brothers went swimming too far out into the sea. They had forgotten about the tides and soon found themselves on a sand bank at low tide, when the fog, like today, rolled in, too thick for them to see their way back. They knew that at high tide their sand bank would be submerged and they could drown. They shouted and screamed until their father found his way to them in his boat and brought them home. Since then, Hans had been wary of the sea, the sand banks and the fog.

He is getting cold standing in the damp spring air, so he goes inside his house. Asbjörn and the crew members who arrived very early this morning are warming themselves by the fire. Hans takes a quick count: only four are still missing. Jensina, his dear wife, has given the men a healthy breakfast of hot barley porridge, served with milk from their cows along with dried apples and berries that she harvested and processed last autumn. Hans can see the toll all this added stress is taking on her. She has been irritable and bad-tempered since giving birth to their second child, a baby girl, just three weeks ago. It was the same two years prior, after she gave birth to their son. Hans thinks that maybe she has the blues. And now, with the new baby in her arms, constantly crying to nurse, she is scrambling to house these men, make their meal and gather enough food supplies for their voyage. Then she tries to calm down their two-year-old, who is having a tantrum from lack of sleep because of all the commotion in the house last night. The little boy badly needs a nap, but there is nowhere to put him down.

'How can I help you?' Hans asks Jensina, gently.

She barely looks at him as she hands him the baby. 'This is too much,' she hisses. 'I really don't want to have to do all this work on top of everything else I have to do around the farm. I'm exhausted.' Before Hans can respond, she continues: 'Do you have any idea if we're going to get compensated for all the food I've gathered for this journey? I've just about used everything we stored for the winter, and it's not even summer yet. Couldn't some of the other men's wives have provided something?'

Hans expresses his sympathy. He knows she is right. Together, they had worked hard to make sure they lacked nothing, but they had not prepared themselves for anything like this. Their supply of food is not endless.

Finally, the last four crew members show up. They apologize for being late. As Hans knew, it had been difficult for them to find their way in the fog. Hans, still with the baby in his arms, invites them in. Jensina gives them whatever is left from the breakfast meal.

'Did you bring your arms?' Hans asks the newcomers. 'Remember you need a spear, an axe and a bow and arrows, and you should also have your own shield?' One man confesses that he only owns an axe. Another says he totally forgot about his armour because he was in such a hurry to leave. Hans curses under his breath and goes to a back room to look for more. Then he remembers the extra set of armour that Asbjörn brought and thanks him when he returns. There are not enough shields, but he says to Asbjörn: 'What you have will have to do.'

Hans gives the baby back to Jensina and calls to the men: 'Off we go now.' He instructs some of the men to carry out the weapons and others to take the provisions, which Jensina has put in bags for them. In the fog, they struggle to make their way to the boathouse, even though it is not far. Together they lift the ship off the wooden planks where it has been resting. Like the other ships in the levy system, it is so light it can be hauled easily over land. They carry it to the shore and place it into the shallow water. The men put the weapons and supplies in the middle of the ship and take their places at the forty oars.

Hans, Asbjörn and two other crew members push the ship out into deeper water. They are soaked up to their waists. Asbjörn and the two men jump aboard. Hans returns to shore. 'Good luck!' he shouts to them and waves as they start rowing away. The timing is fortunate, he thinks. It is high tide, so the crew does not have to worry about the sand banks.

Hans walks back to the farmhouse, where he finds Jensina washing the bowls and cleaning up, still with the baby in her arms. Their little boy is now fast asleep on one of the benches. Now the men have gone and the farmhouse is theirs again, Hans can see his wife is beginning to relax, but not entirely. 'How on earth are they going to find their way in this fog?' she asks. 'I suspect we'll have them back here in a day or two.'

Hans nods. Again, he thinks she may be right. 'For now,' he says, 'you just get some rest. I'll take care of the clean-up after I've helped our farmhands milk the cows and feed the pigs.'

Jensina was right. The crew on Hans' ship did return because they were not able to find the other ships in the fog. On their way back, after the fog had lifted, they heard from fishermen that the summons from the king's envoy was a false alarm and the expedition had been called off. Hans and Jensina were elated to see their neighbours and relatives return unharmed – and relieved to get most of their food back.

3RD HOUR OF THE DAY
(08.00–09.00)

A SON BURIES HIS
REVENANT FATHER

Arnkel Thorolfsson sets off from Bolstad, his farm, with eleven men, a sled and digging tools because his late father, Thorolf Bjarnarson, is no longer 'lying quietly in his grave' but is terrorizing the district. Arnkel knows it is his responsibility to solve the problem, and there is only one way to do it – dig up his father's remains and bury them somewhere else, safely farther away.

Arnkel has no choice. He has received many complaints from his neighbours and friends that Thorolf, nicknamed Lame-Foot, is haunting the area. They told him the oxen used to haul Thorolf to his grave were now ridden by trolls, that any birds landing on Thorolf's cairn immediately fell down dead and that any livestock that came even near his grave would run wild and bellow themselves to death. People feared for their lives, too. Things had become so bad most people dared not go outside after sunset. They claimed that during the night they had often heard loud noises at Thorolf's old farm, Hvam, and sometimes people were scared that the revenants – other people who had died as a result of Thorolf's hauntings – were sitting on the roofs of their own buildings.

Ghosts in medieval Iceland are often depicted as malevolent, brutal and vengeful. Their relationship with the living was seldom peaceful. While alive the ones who returned as ghosts after death were usually disliked and unpopular people.

The shepherd at Hvam would often run home with his flock, claiming he was being chased by Thorolf. Then, one evening, he and his livestock did not return. The next morning, the group searching for the missing shepherd discovered his body, black all over and with all his bones broken, only a short distance from Thorolf's cairn. Arnkel had the shepherd's body buried quickly beside Thorolf. Some of the shepherd's livestock were found dead too, while the rest appeared to have strayed into the mountains, never to be found again. During the winter, Thorolf began to appear inside his old home, where he pursued the mistress of the house. His nocturnal visits became so troublesome that she lost her mind and eventually

STONE CAIRNS WERE USED TO MARK THE BURIAL SPOTS OF THE DEAD IN THE VIKING AGE. THIS CAIRN IS LOCATED IN ONE OF THE BEST-PRESERVED NORSE RUINS IN GREENLAND.

died of insanity. She was carried to Thorsardale and buried beside Thorolf, but that did not keep him quiet in his grave. He started to roam widely around the valley, devastating farms and killing some men who were later seen walking with him on his hauntings. People became so frightened they began to flee the area.

At times, Arnkel had invited people to stay with him, because wherever he was, there was no trouble from Thorolf and his revenant companions. But Arnkel knew he could not be everywhere at once, so he finally decided Thorolf's body must be moved for the good of the district. In the early spring, when the earth was beginning to thaw, he sent a messenger to the sons of Thorbrand at Karsstadir to ask them to help move Thorolf out of Thorsardale and find a burial site further away. At first they declined, saying they did not see any need to help, even though Icelandic law said that anyone who is asked has a duty to rebury the dead people in a new grave. After their father scolded them for disobeying the law, one of Thorbrand's sons, Thorodd, told the messenger he would assist Arnkel on behalf of his brothers.

Arnkel and his eleven men now ride to the farm at Ulfarsfell, where they meet Thorodd Thorbrandsson and two of his men at the agreed-upon time. By now, everyone in the group is keenly aware of Arnkel's problem. Though they are sympathetic and willing to help him, Arnkel can tell they are clearly not looking forward to their gruesome and perhaps dangerous task.

From Ulfarsfell, they ride up along the ridge and into Thorsardale, where Thorolf is buried. They find the cairn littered with dead birds. Scattered about are the carcasses of cows and sheep. The quiet is so eerie that not even the wind dares to make a sound. The men nervously set out to work, breaking open Thorolf's cairn with their digging tools. They freeze in fear when they break open the mound and see Thorolf's body, which has not decomposed but has become hideous to look at – his eyes are wide open with the same menacing look he took with him to the grave, while his fingernails are curled into claws, his hair long and unkempt, his beard reaching down to his chest. Strangest of all, his body is black as pitch and so swollen he looks more like a troll than a human.

No one wants to go near him, much less touch him, but they know he must be moved, for the good of the people and animals in the valley. When they touch him, however, they find Thorolf so heavy that it takes several men to lift him out of his grave. After several long pauses to gather their strength, they manage to place him on the sled. From there, they begin to haul him up along the ridge towards Ulfarsfellshals, but Thorodd's strong oxen soon become so exhausted they must be replaced by two others to continue.

Arnkel's plan is to rebury Thorolf's body at Vadilshöfdi, but when they come to the edge of the ridge the two oxen break free and run wild. Arnkel, Thorodd and the other men watch as the oxen run down the ridge, charge out along the hillside near the farm at Ulfarsfell and then out to the foreshore. 'Ride after them to see where they're going,' Arnkel tells one of his men. When he returns a little later, he reports that both oxen had collapsed and died. By now, Thorolf is heavier still. It takes all the men to drag him onto his sled and to a small headland nearby, where they can dispose of him and build a cairn covered with heavy stones. Arnkel promises his companions that he will make arrangements to have a stone wall built across the headland above the cairn immediately – a wall so high no one except a bird in flight could ever see over it.

Arnkel is greatly relieved that his revenant father has finally been put to rest, even though in life Arnkel had considered him an immoral, unpleasant, scheming man. The day before his death, in fact, Thorolf had tried to make amends with his son. He arrived at Bolstad, where Arnkel gave him a warm welcome and asked, 'What brought you here?' It was obvious to Arnkel that his father was in a very bad mood, though he was trying hard to conceal it.

'My reason for coming', said Thorolf, 'is that I don't like it that we're not getting along. I'd like to put that behind us and renew our kinship. With your courage and my plans, it seems to me that we can become the most powerful men in the district.' Thorolf went on to explain to him his concerns about the Krakunes Woods and his fall-out with the chieftain Snorri Thorgrimsson at Helgafell. Thorolf had lent the woods to Snorri to use for his own purposes as part of an earlier legal settlement, but he felt Snorri exploited the woods, treating them as entirely his own. So, earlier that day he had ridden over to Helgafell to confront the other man. Snorri did not agree with Thorolf's assessment and was not willing to give up the woods, claiming the matter could only be cleared up by seeking the opinion of those who had witnessed the deal. 'I suggest', Thorolf then said to Arnkel, 'that we begin our reconciliation by getting back Krakunes Woods from Snorri. I feel that he oppresses us, and his claims about the woods are false. He's a complete liar.'

Arnkel knew his father well enough not to be tricked into something like this. He pointed out that it had not been out of friendship that his father lent the woods to Snorri. 'I'm not going to involve myself in a dispute with him,' said Arnkel. 'I know very well that Snorri doesn't have any legal rights to the woods, but I don't want you gloating over a quarrel between him and me.'

Thorolf was furious, left abruptly and rode home in a huff.

Arnkel could not have known this conversation would be their last. In retrospect, he wishes they had parted on better terms, for the next morning a messenger came to Arnkel, telling him that after Thorolf's return from Bolstad he had placed himself in his high seat at Hvam, refused to speak to anyone and declined all offers of food. By the next morning, said the messenger, Thorolf was still sitting upright in his high seat – but was now dead. The servants were frightened by the sight of him, especially the menacing look on his face.

Arnkel immediately rode over to Hvam with some of his men to confirm that his father had indeed died. When Arnkel got there and entered the fire-room, he found it empty except for his father, still sitting in the same position. He invited his men to join him but warned them not to walk in front of Thorolf until he had closed his father's eyes. Arnkel walked along the benches behind his father and took hold of his shoulders. Arnkel was astonished by how much force it took to move him. He wrapped cloth around Thorolf's head and prepared his body for burial, instructing the men in the house to break down the wall behind Thorolf so he could move the corpse outside.

Arnkel thought he could carry his father alone, but he soon found him to be too heavy and needed help from two other men. Meanwhile, two oxen were harnessed to a sled that would carry Thorolf's corpse. Though straining with much effort, the oxen eventually managed to pull the makeshift hearse to Thorsardale, which Arnkel had chosen as an appropriate place for the burial. There, Arnkel and his men tipped Thorolf off the sled, heaped a mound of soil over his corpse and buried him beneath a strong cairn built of heavy stone. There had been no formal funeral procession because Arnkel knew very well that his father was unpopular; no one would join in, and certainly no one would miss him. After the burial, Arnkel rode to Hvam and claimed as his own all his father's property and possessions. He stayed for three nights, then went back to Bolstad.

For the rest of Arnkel's life, his father rested quietly in his new grave, but when Arnkel died Thorolf broke out once more. He began to terrorize people in the district and do so much damage that people realized they had to open his grave and move him yet again. Because he was now even heavier than before, they were only able to drag Thorolf to the brink of the headland, where they dropped him on the beach, kindled a fire and burned his body. But even this was not the end of him. A lean cow soon went down to the beach where the corpse had been burned and licked the stones onto which his ashes had drifted. The cow later gave birth to a bull calf, dapple-grey and of abnormal size and strength. Long before the calf was fully grown, it gored its master to death and ran away, only to sink in a marsh and never be seen again – marking the end, finally, of Thorolf.

A RUNE MASTER UNVEILS HIS WORK OF ART

It is a big day for Balli, because today he gets to unveil his rune stone. Other than his immediate family, very few people call him by his birth name but instead refer to him as Erilar, rune master. This morning, Balli has had a healthy breakfast with his wife and children, finished chores around his farm and now changes into his best clothes and asks his wife and children to do the same. His family has never seen the rune stone, even though he has been working on it for three to four hours almost every day for about two years. In the spring and summer, he has put in even more hours because he prefers to work in broad daylight and with the sun at a particular angle. There is a high demand for memorial rune stones in Sweden, especially in Uppland, and Balli gets so many commissions that sometimes he has to decline the work.

He learned the futhark (the runic alphabet) and the skill of carving runes from his father, who in turn learned it from his father. Balli is deeply grateful to his father because being a rune master has become more lucrative for him than farming. He prefers to carve on stone, but sometimes he carves runes on wood for free for friends and relatives who need ownership tags for their trading goods or want to send messages to family members or acquaintances.

Runes are the individual letters of the runic alphabet, the oldest and only native system of writing used by the Germanic peoples. This alphabet is called the futhark after its first letters. Each rune had a fixed place in the order of the alphabet and a name that was also a meaningful word.

It was around two years ago when Vidhugsi, a wealthy farmer in the neighbourhood, came to Balli's farm, announcing with sadness that his father had passed away from old age. He asked Balli to help him commemorate his father with an elaborate rune stone. Vidhugsi told him that after an intense search, he had found a suitable granite boulder along two paths that cross between his and a neighbouring village: the perfect place, he said, where the inscription could be seen by many people. Together, they went to look at the stone. After careful examination, Balli said he was indeed impressed with both the location and the stone – large and almost round, except for one side that was nearly flat and ideal for carving.

Vidhugsi was very specific to Balli about what he wanted inscribed:

> *Vidhugsi had this stone erected for Særeif, his good father. He lived at Ågersta. Here the stone shall stand between the villages*

Vidhugsi was also clear about how these words were to appear. He wanted something special, something different from most other memorial rune stones in the district, with their inscriptions in two or three straight lines. In fact, he had a unique memorial stone design in mind and tried to explain it to Balli. To make sure he understood Vidhugsi's vision, Balli used his sharp knife to scratch on a slab of wood two interlaced dragon-snakes with some flourishes – the runic text could appear inside the bodies of the snakes. Vidhugsi was very pleased with the design. 'It's exactly what I want,' he said, then paid Balli a handsome sum of money. The two shook hands to close the deal.

After accepting the job, Balli began to feel overwhelmed by the challenge. 'After all, I'm a rune master, not an artist,' he thought to himself, but he had been unable to resist accepting the large payment. Balli is also aware that fashions are changing, and wealthy customers like Vidhugsi are no longer satisfied with simple, short epigraphs. He suspects that on his travels throughout Sweden and Denmark, Vidhugsi had seen some elaborate monumental rune stones, maybe even the two famous Jelling stones in Jutland. Balli has not seen them himself, but the larger of the two Jelling stones has been described to him as a magnificent piece of work with three sides, two of which have relief carving of a crucified Christ and a lion entwined with a snake.

Balli started work on his new project right away. Most mornings, he would walk to the stone, carrying the two tools he needed for carving, a chisel and hammer made by a local blacksmith. His chisel is a metal shaft with an angled blunt end. His hammer has a wooden shaft and a solid iron head. To carve, he pounds on the chisel to create indents in the stone. He is very careful not to hit the chisel too hard, for it could crack the stone or leave unwanted indent marks – something he has learned from years of experience. He has also learned not to rush because once while working on Vighugsi's stone he was in such a hurry that he mishit the end of the chisel with his hammer. Fortunately, it did not leave a glaring mark or indent on his work, only a slight mistake that he hoped no one, especially Vighugsi, would notice – though he did smash his thumb so badly he could not work on the rune stone for some weeks.

Before he went home at the end of each workday, he always covered the stone with a linen cloth, securing it with a rope tied at the bottom so it would not blow off with the wind. He knows the stone is very solid, and his carvings are deep, so strong wind and foul weather do not concern him. However, he does fear that another rune master might appropriate his elaborate design or that possible enemies of Vidhugsi or his late father in the district might vandalize the stone.

Balli started by carving the lines of the two interlaced dragon-snakes that would fill the entire flat side of the stone, but progress was slow. 'This is taking forever,' he mumbled to himself. At times, he even felt like giving up, especially after he hurt his thumb. But Balli is a man of his word, and telling Vidhugsi that he was unable to finish the job would be too humiliating. Also, he had already spent a good portion of Vidhugsi's payment on renovating his farmhouse and would not have the means to pay him back. Balli's mood brightened considerably when he finally finished the outlines of the two dragon-snakes and could begin carving the runes inside their bodies:

• uiþugsi • lit raisa - stain • þiasn iftiR • seref faþur sen • koþan •han • byki • agurstam • hier mn • stanta • miþli • bua

Balli likes to put dots in his inscriptions between each word, rather than create one long word like some rune masters, which makes the runes harder to read. With or without dots, carving such a long inscription has not been easy. Although he is well acquainted with the runic alphabet, the futhark, there were times when he was not sure which runic letter to use because a single letter can denote several sounds. For example, the futhark has no sign for *e*, *o*, *d* and *p*, and the *k* rune is used for both *k* and *g*. Sometimes, he would spend sleepless nights pondering which runic character he should use to represent a sound. But now, that part of the job was complete.

Although he had tried to space the words in such a way that they would fill the entire bodies of the two dragon-snakes, there was some space left on one of the bodies when he was done. 'It looks too empty here,' he thought. Not knowing exactly what to do with the empty space, he summoned Vidhugsi. Balli suggested that maybe he could add his own signature – after all, this stone was *his* masterpiece – and much to his delight Vidhugsi liked the idea. Balli carefully measured the space left in the dragon-snake's body and proudly carved his finishing touches:

raþi • tekr • þaR • rynsi • runum • þim sum • bali • risti

Let any man skilled in runes read the runes that Balli carved

Now, on the day of the stone's unveiling, Balli is starting to feel irritated because his little family has taken a long time to dress and get ready. Finally, they make their way to Ågersta. It is not a long walk, but two of his children are very young and sometimes need to rest. Balli begins to worry they may be late, thinking perhaps it was not a good idea to bring his family along. But he badly wants his older sons to see his masterpiece and hopes it will inspire them to learn the runes and the art of carving on stone. Balli picks up one of his young children and his wife the other so they can walk faster and make better time. They even manage to arrive before the agreed-upon time. One of Balli's young children immediately runs to the stone and tries to peek underneath the linen cloth, but his wife snatches up the child before he can. Balli relaxes and sees Vidhugsi approaching, leading a large group of people, whom Balli believes to be Vidhugsi's immediate and extended family. The crowd gathers around the stone in a large ceremonial circle. Walking up to the stone, Vidhugsi asks Balli to join him and then addresses the gathering:

'We are here to celebrate the life and achievements of my father Særeif, the best and most accomplished man I have ever known. Let us now take a brief moment in silence to remember him.' After a short while, the crowd begins to murmur, breaking the silence as they are eager to see the new memorial. Vidhugsi asks Balli to unveil the stone, so he begins to untie the knots that hold the cloth covering the rune stone, pausing briefly to reflect on the many hours he has spent working on it. He knows its shape and surface as well as a mother would know her own child. The work of art is his child.

When he finally throws off the linen cloth he hears gasps and then the applause of the crowd, who rush to the stone to touch it and congratulate Vidhugsi and Balli on their masterpiece. Above the din, Vidhugsi turns to Balli and thanks him for having undertaken such a difficult job, then points to a field nearby, where two teenage boys stand with four cows. 'These are now your cows,' Vighugsi announces. 'You followed my directions, but I'd never thought the stone would turn out to be so phenomenal. You've created the most beautiful memorial stone in the whole district.'

BALLI'S MASTERPIECE. THE UPPLAND RUNIC INSCRIPTIONS ARE FAMOUS EXAMPLES OF VIKING AGE RUNIC STONES AND OFFER VITAL INFORMATION FOR OUR KNOWLEDGE OF VIKING SOCIETY.

Vidhugsi's family brings out ale and delicious food to the delight of the people, now seated on the grass around the rune stone. Balli sits down next to Vidhugsi; there is one last thing he wants to suggest as a finishing touch on the memorial stone – painting the inscription, as some rune masters outside of Uppland have done. Although Balli has never painted inscriptions before, he would like to start with this one, and he has done his research. He explains that the most common colours are red and black paint, derived from red lead and soot. Other options are red ochre, also very common, and calcium carbonate (white), both of which are relatively inexpensive because they can be locally made, though their colours tend of wash off fairly quickly. White lead, green malachite and blue azure are also available, explains Balli, but they are more expensive, as they have to be imported. Vidhugsi gently shakes his head, telling Balli he is happy with the stone just as it is.

They shake hands again, and Balli starts looking for his family. He is feeling a little tipsy from all the ale, but eventually he manages to find them and tells them to stay put while he proudly gathers the four cows gifted to him by his patron.

5TH HOUR OF THE DAY
(10.00–11.00)

A LAWSPEAKER
ANNOUNCES
A NEW LAW

Thorgeir Thorkelsson, a prominent chieftain from Ljosavatn in the north of Iceland, emerges from his booth – a square space dug into the ground with tarpaulin for cover in case of rain. But it is not raining today. In fact, the weather is glorious. It is the ninth week of summer, and the sun sets for only about an hour each day now. He looks around to admire this amazing place – Thingvellir – the site of the Althing, the Icelandic Parliament. He is well acquainted with the place because he is one of thirty-five chieftains (*godar*) who must attend the Althing along with their thingmen, their followers and supporters, for about two weeks at this time each year.

THE LAW ROCK WAS THE PLACE FROM WHICH LAWS WERE PROCLAIMED.

Yet Thorgeir cannot help but be awed by the beauty of the place every time he comes. Earthquakes have created rifts in the landscape to form a dramatic high rock wall. Receding down from this wall is a grassy hillside and below that spreads out a broad grassy plain. He knows that when one stands at the top of the hill with their back to the rock wall, their voice will be heard far out over the plain because the acoustics are just that perfect. From this rock, the so-called the Law Rock, he has heard many of the country's laws proclaimed.

The law-speaker, the state's highest and only secular official, was elected by the chieftains for a three-year term. He was annually required to recite one third of the laws at the Law Rock. In this way, the entire body of law was proclaimed over a three-year cycle.

Further out on this plain, the legislative court meets to debate the laws of the land and other business. Several of his fellow chieftains, who come from all over the country, have brought their families with them as usual. It is likely that in the day and evening before the start of the Althing, there had been trading, family visiting and the playing of games. Thorgeir is disappointed his wife could not be with him this year. Even though it would have been a very long trip on horseback for her, she would have loved to see her many friends and relatives again.

But these are not normal times. Thorgeir has a lot on his mind today. Despite the outward appearance of so much goodwill among the people gathered here, the underlying mood of the people at the Althing does not reflect the tranquillity and beauty of Thingvellir. Indeed, there are huge tensions among his fellow citizens. Thorgeir is even worried that a civil war could break out – an outcome that would divide his lovely country in two.

The issue that is cutting so deeply is religion. Like his forebears, Thorgeir is a Heathen, one who does not believe in the god or gods of any of the major religions, including Christianity. In fact, as a chieftain (*godi*) he has had little choice in the matter. Among his many and varied duties, he has had to maintain the local great hall where community members hold their heathen feasts and religious observances. Many times, he has conducted and presided over these Heathen religious rites, even though his heart was not always in it. Unlike some of his countrymen, Thorgeir is not an avid believer. He is definitely not a religious fanatic. Does he truly believe in Thor, Odin, Njörd, Frey, Freyja, Frigg and the other Heathen gods and goddesses? He has pondered this question many times and admits that he is not sure. For him, the pagan religious observances have become merely a tradition to follow. He is aware that a new religion has come to Iceland and that some of his countrymen have already embraced Christianity, but he is pragmatic and just wants the best for his country and its citizens, even if that means having to convert to Christianity and abandon some of his family traditions. He wonders, though, how he will be able to swear the oath of the chieftains if he were to become a Christian and worries if he will be excluded from some important businesses at home in Ljosavatn and at the Althing if he were to convert.

With so much on his mind, Thorgeir has not slept since his arrival at Thingvellir; he is exhausted. He also feels unkempt and grubby because he has not had the time to wash or even to change his clothes and trim his beard. He has been too busy because he has been tasked with an important role: that of law-speaker, the ultimate decision of whether the country remains Heathen or turns to Christianity resting on his shoulders. Those who had already converted to Christianity had wanted chieftain Hall Thorsteinsson from Sida to make the decision. Hall had been actively introducing Christianity into Iceland and had proposed new laws in agreement with the Christian faith. But when the Heathens offered Hall the prestigious office of law-speaker, he declined because he did not want to accept the responsibility of possibly dividing the state. When Thorgeir was then approached to resolve the conflict, he had reluctantly agreed. With the fate of the entire country now resting in his hands, Thorgeir decides he needs peace and quiet to think. Rather than unwind with his fellow chieftains, friends and members of his and his wife's family, he withdraws to his booth, puts a fur blanket over his head to keep away the noise and commotion around him and spends all night meditating, concentrating on how to find a solution.

His time alone proves fruitful. By the next morning, Thorgeir has made up his mind and decided what needs to be done. He walks from his booth across the grassy plain, up the hill and climbs up to the Law Rock. He calls out to all the people at the Althing to gather round. They are eager to hear him and immediately start to assemble. He looks out over the large crowd and recognizes Hjalti Skeggjason and Gissur Teitsson among the many people who are clearly in favour of adopting the Christian faith. There is a man standing right next to them who he does not know, though Thorgeir thinks he may be a Christian priest whom they have brought along from Norway. He has not seen Hjalti and Gissur for a while. Hjalti had been sentenced to three years of exile for composing and reciting an offensive lampoon at the Althing, in which he had denounced the pagan gods and called the goddess Freyja a bitch. Because of his three-year exile, Hjalti had gone to

Norway with Gissur, his father-in-law, to consult with King Olaf Tryggvason, a relative of Gissur. Thorgeir does not know all the details of the visit, but he heard that King Olaf was furious about how one of his missionary priests, Thangbrand, had been mistreated in Iceland. He also heard the king was angry that Icelanders were so reluctant to adopt Christianity and had threatened to maim, even kill, any Icelanders who happened to be in Norway. Hjalti and Gissur, both firm Christians, had managed to dissuade King Olaf in return for his permission to go back to Iceland and plead the cause of Christianity at the Althing.

Because the pro-Christian party before him now is so large, Thorgeir suspects the two were carefully carrying out their plan yesterday before the commencement of the Althing. He believes they sent out secret messages to the members of the assembly, asking all sympathizers of the Christian faith to join them en masse today. He is nevertheless surprised to see Hjalti at the Althing – because of his outlawry, Hjalti is not supposed to be allowed to visit the site of the assembly. In the past, he would have objected to Hjalti's presence, but not today. This is no time, he thinks, to dwell on something that suddenly seems so trivial.

When everyone has finally gathered, Thorgeir begins to talk. He feels well prepared because he spent the early hours of the morning rehearsing his speech again and again; he chooses his words carefully. He begins by giving a warning: the people of Iceland must live under the same single set of laws or chaos will ensue, he says. The people cannot survive under two differing sets of laws, which will only lead to disagreements, disturbances and eventually lay waste the entire country. 'I don't want that to happen,' he says.

He cites the kings of Norway and Denmark, who had fought for so long that the people in both countries eventually tired of the warfare and intervened to arrange peace between the two kings. The people were so successful that the kings would eventually send gifts to each other, and the peace lasted for as long as the two kings had lived. 'It seems to me', Thorgeir goes on to say, 'that we do not let those prevail who are most strongly opposed to one another. Rather let us come to a compromise between them so that each party may win a part of its case. We need to have one law and one faith. Believe me, if we sunder the law, we will sunder the peace.' So he declares that all people in Iceland shall have one law and one religion – and announces that the religion shall be the Christian faith.

He takes his time to study the faces of the people gathered at Thingvellir. He can tell from the expressions that those in the Heathen party are displeased, some even shocked, that he, a pagan at least in name, could make such a decision. He senses that they feel betrayed and quickly realizes he must make some concessions to appease them. So, he announces that he will allow people to continue the practice of exposing infants before they have been given a name, though he knows this will not go down well with the Christians, for whom the exposure of an unbaptized child means sending the child to the devil. Thorgeir is not in favour of this practice either, but he believes that under certain circumstances – if the baby is deformed or very sick, or if the parents are very poor – it is a practical thing to do. He also allows people to continue eating horse meat, a food especially common among the poor but forbidden for Christians. Finally, he allows the people to worship the old gods, so long as they do so in strict secret. He is thinking here primarily of the older generation, wanting to make their transition from the old religion to the new as smooth as possible. He warns, however, that this practice will be punished by a three-year exile if witnesses are ever produced.

From this moment on, Christianity is the law of the land in Iceland, which means everyone must be baptized. As Thorgeir climbs down from the Law Rock, he sees that the priests are already preparing the ceremony for those in attendance. Not everyone, however, likes the idea of being plunged into the cold water of the River Öxara at Thingvellir. Thorgeir is not thrilled about being baptized there either, but he feels he needs to set a good example, so he subjects himself to a cold-water dip before he rides home. Some people flatly refuse and promise instead to get baptized in the hot springs on their way home from the Althing. Thorgeir wonders if they will fulfil their promises, but he decides that is not his problem. He has done what he was asked to do.

Thorgeir would never know that his speech, delivered in the year 1000, would later become the most famous speech in Icelandic history.

6TH HOUR OF THE DAY
(11.00–12.00)

A SLAVE WOMAN
BREAKS HER SILENCE

Melkorka is sitting on a small knoll by the stream that runs down the slope of the hayfield beneath Höskuldsstadir. It is a beautiful summer day as she watches her darling son, Olaf, play in the grass below. This is not only her favourite outdoor place, but it has also become her and Olaf's secret place, where they can spend time together away from others and chat – the only person she can chat to. Although he is only two years old, Olaf is a gifted child with the agility and speech of a four-year-old. She is enormously proud of him and can hardly take her eyes off her handsome son, but she is getting sleepy and is about to lean back to soak in the sunshine and close her eyes for a few minutes, when he runs up to her.

In his little hand he is carrying a dandelion that has lost its bloom. 'Look, Mum, look what I found!' he says. She laughs, gives him a hug, takes the dandelion, which is clearly intended as her present, and gently places him on her knees. She then teaches him to blow the billowing tufts of the dandelion seed heads. 'If you can clear all the wispy seeds in one strong breath, you can make a wish,' she tells him. He blows as hard as he can, but does not quite manage it this first time, so the two walk off to look for more fluffy white dandelions. After a few minutes, they return to the knoll with a handful. Olaf blows again and again, hoping to earn the right to make a wish. Melkorka asks him what he will wish for when he succeeds. She is not surprised to learn that Olaf can voice many wishes, from a new pair of skates to use when the lakes freeze to having his own horse and, one day, his own ship.

Olaf wants to know what his mother would wish for. Melkorka cannot share her real wish with Olaf, for she would ask for a different life for herself, something that he would be too young to understand. For now, to make him feel happy, she says she would wish for some new clothes and maybe a good meal when they return to the house. Olaf knows nothing about her tragic past. He doesn't know that when she was fifteen years old, she was captured as a slave by Vikings in Ireland. The experience was so traumatic she decided she would never utter a single word again. After she had been held in captivity for some time, Gilli the Russian, a slave-trader, bought her from the Vikings. Gilli took her and eleven other slave women to the Brenno Islands, where there was a large assembly of chieftains and traders from different lands. Melkorka was terrified by the din coming from the loud festivities, where she could see crowds of men drinking and playing games.

Gilli led her and the other women to a decorative tent some distance away from the other booths. He told them to take off all their clothes except for their underwear and to sit in a row across the width of the tent. Melkorka chose to sit at the end of the row. Gilli then drew an inner curtain across the tent, evidently so no one entering the tent could see that he was selling slave women. A couple of hours later, a Norseman walked in. Melkorka heard him introduce himself as Höskuld Kolsson and say to Gilli that he wanted to buy a slave woman. Gilli said he had nothing like that for sale, but Höskuld clearly did not believe him, because he pulled the inner curtain aside. He stood at the entrance and began to look down the row at the dozen scantily clad women, as if he were judging cattle. He panned right then left a couple of times. Melkorka could feel that his eyes had settled on her at the end of the row. His stare made her feel so uncomfortable that she began to feel naked, so she folded her arms to hide her breasts and crossed her legs. She was not surprised when she heard Höskuld ask Gilli how much she would cost him. Gilli said he wanted three marks of silver, but Höskuld said, 'That's too much, too expensive. Why, I could buy three slave women for that price.' Gilli tried to argue that she was special, that she was worth more than the other women, but then he had to admit that she had a major flaw – she could not speak. 'I've tried to speak with her in many ways,' Melkorka heard Gilli say to Höskuld, 'but I never got so much as a word from her.' He encouraged Höskuld to look at the other eleven women again – pick one and he could have her for one mark of silver. But Höskuld had made up his mind. He wanted Melkorka. Höskuld asked Gilli to weigh the silver coins in the purse he carried on his belt to see if he had enough. Melkorka would never forget the sound of Höskuld's coins clinking on Gilli's scales. She wanted to scream out, 'I am a person! I am not an object that you can buy and sell for your pieces of silver!' Her silent screams went unheard, however. It soon became clear that Höskuld had the right amount of money. She saw the two of them shake hands to seal the deal. She cast a long glance at the other slave women, who seemed to be gesturing with their eyes, wishing her the best of luck. Höskuld, her master now, went to her, took her hand and led her to his booth.

When they got to Höskuld's booth, Melkorka could feel the nerves in her stomach. She did not know what to expect from her master, but when she looked at him more carefully she began to console herself. He did not look anything like the brutish men who had abducted her and many other women back home in Ireland. In fact, she found him quite handsome. He then offered her delicious food and provided her with a comfortable place to sleep on the ground in the booth. When Höskuld had left his tent to socialize, she devoured the food and soon fell fast asleep.

During the night, she woke to find him lying next to her. She remembers being scared, but his strong, warm body felt comforting. He gently took her head in his hands and kissed her cheeks, then her mouth and then her breasts. It was the first time she had ever lain with a man. The intercourse hurt a little – she found a few spots of blood on the bed cloth the next morning – but she had been fortunate. It had not been unpleasant, not at all the way she had heard the other slave women describe it. When she and Höskuld dressed the next morning, he looked at her clothes and shook his head, opened a chest from which he took some fine women's clothing and gave them to her. As he had done the day before, he took her hand and the two walked to the assembly. She could tell by the way people looked at her that they were impressed with her appearance.

The next day, Höskuld took her home with him to Iceland. The ship landed at the mouth of the Laxa River, where he had the cargo unloaded and the ship drawn up on the beach on the inland side. She heard him tell some men to construct a boat shed for the ship and to transport the timber to his farm, to be completed before he got there. He made her sit behind him on his horse – in her view, a pony – with her arms wrapped firmly around him so she would not fall off. The horse started off in a gallop, but when he felt her squeeze his waist very tightly, he slowed the horse's gait to a walk. She later learned that Icelandic horses are unique because they have five gaits. They walk, trot, gallop, tölt and fly pace. The two received a warm welcome when they arrived at Höskuld's farm, but when he introduced Melkorka to his wife, Jorun, she was not happy. 'Who is this woman?' Jorun asked.

'Believe me, I don't know her name, because she cannot speak,' he answered. Then he told Jorun how he had acquired her.

'Alright, I'm not about to wrangle with you over a slave woman who is both deaf and dumb,' she said. 'You probably

wasted a lot of money, but I'll find work for her to do.'
Melkorka was surprised how a man as handsome and gentle
as Höskuld could have picked Jorun as his wife, who was not
only unattractive but also coarse in her speech and manners.

Melkorka often felt disappointed that Höskuld never came
to her bed again. There were nights when she would lie awake
missing that one night in the Brenno Islands and longing for
his warm embrace again. In fact, she hardly ever saw him over
the next several months. It was not until late winter when she
had given birth to a boy, and Höskuld had been summoned
to give the boy a name, that he would spend any time in her
company. He decided to name the child Olaf after his uncle,
Olaf Feilan Thorsteinsson, who had died recently. She heard
him say to the women who helped with the birth that he had
never seen a more handsome or more distinguished-looking
child.

Melkorka looked at him, hoping that he would at least
acknowledge her existence, but he avoided her eyes. After the
birth of Olaf, however, Melkorka saw more of Höskuld, though
his visits were primarily to spend time with their son. She could
tell Höskuld was very fond of him. Jorun, however, clearly did
not like her and always assigned her unpleasant tasks around
the farm, such as washing people's dirty clothes in the brook
and cleaning the farmhouse. She showed no interest in Olaf
whatsoever. Melkorka did not know if Höskuld had told Jorun
about that night on the island, but she suspected they must
have had a serious discussion, because on Olaf's first birthday
Höskuld announced that from now on her only job would be
waiting upon both him and Jorun, and taking care of Olaf.

Back at the knoll with her son, Melkorka suddenly hears footsteps behind her. She turns to see Höskuld only a few feet away. 'I was doing some farm work,' he says, 'but then I heard voices and followed the sound and found the two of you here. You can clearly talk, as you have plenty to say to our boy. Tell me your name.' Höskuld takes hold of Olaf and places the boy on his knees, but the boy cannot sit still. He is obsessed with the dandelions and insists that Höskuld blow the tufts of the dandelion seed heads and make wishes. 'Go get us some more,' Höskuld says to Olaf and lets him run off. Melkorka takes a deep breath and replies: 'Alright then, I'll tell you. My name is Melkorka.' Höskuld nods as if in deep thought and looks at her for some time. 'Tell me about your family,' he says. She looks away for a while before she answers: 'My father is Myrkjartan, a king in Ireland. I was taken captive there at the age of fifteen.' Höskuld gets up abruptly and asks, 'How could you possibly have concealed such a noble birth from me?' He walks back to the farmhouse before Melkorka has a chance to answer and explain.

Melkorka does not know what to think, so she fetches Olaf and walks home with him to do her chores. When she enters the house, she can tell by the expression on Jorun's face that she is in a very bad mood. The wife sits down on one of the benches and instructs Melkorka to kneel down; she is to remove Jorun's socks and shoes and place them on the floor. This is a new assignment for Melkorka, because until now Jorun has always dressed and undressed herself. As soon as Melkorka is done, Jorun picks up the socks and strikes her in the face with them. It does not hurt, but Melkorka flies into a rage. She has had enough. Over the years, she has suffered many humiliations, but never before has anyone struck her. Before she can think, she gives Jorun a blow on the nose with her right fist and sees with pleasure that it causes a nosebleed.

Jorun screams for help and Höskuld comes running in to separate the two women. He calls for a servant woman to wipe the blood from Jorun's nose. Meanwhile, Melkorka stares at her own fist with surprise and rubs it with her left hand. It was a hard blow. The way that Jorun is acting, she wonders if the wife's nose is broken. 'I can't believe that a slave woman has hit me,' Jorun shouts. 'Get rid of her at once!' Höskuld quicky grabs Melkorka by the arm and leads her outside. 'You have to realize that you can no longer stay here,' he says. 'I'll arrange for you and Olaf to move to another farm.' Melkorka is delighted with the offer, goes inside and promptly gathers her and Olaf's few belongings. She hopes she will never have to deal with Jorun again.

Höskuld kept his promise. He moved Melkorka and Olaf to a farm further up the valley on the south shore of the river. She set up household there, called Melkorkustadir. Höskuld supplied her and Olaf with everything they needed until he felt that Olaf was old enough to look after his mother's affairs. It is ironic that once Höskuld decided to turn over his responsibilities to Olaf, Melkorka's feelings for Höskuld, once so warm, cooled.

A MAN IS ACCUSED OF BEING HOMOSEXUAL

Njal Thorgeirsson's foster son, Höskuld Thrainsson, has been killed by Njal's three biological sons – Skarphedin, Helgi and Grim – and wergild must be paid as compensation for the killing.

Wergild (literally 'man-payment' and sometimes referred to as blood money) is the monetary value that was established for a person's life or injuries, to be paid as a fine or as compensatory damages to the person's family if that person was killed or injured by another.

So far, wise and influential men from all over Iceland have managed to avert the blood vengeance which would have thrown powerful families into conflict and led to the death of many good men. A compensation plan is now in place. At the Althing, a settlement is to be concluded with a very large sum of money. The silver is now collected into a pile, awaiting the time when the adversaries of Njal's sons are to come and retrieve it. The main adversaries are Flosi Thordarson and the sons of Sigfus, who are all in one way or another related to Höskuld. The leader, Flosi, is the uncle of Hildigun, the deceased Höskuld's wife.

Flosi cannot believe that he has been dragged into this family feud, and he resents it. He is a Christian and considers himself an even-tempered man. Violence, whether physical or verbal, is not in his nature. His parents, Thord and Ingun, had always been loving and kind to him and his half-brother. He was raised in an atmosphere of tranquillity and has dutifully followed the family's Christian moral values ever since. He has always lived a peaceful life as a farmer and a powerful chieftain in Svinafell. He and his wife, Steinvör, with whom he has a son, both get along well with the people in his district. He treats his thingmen well and knows that has earned their respect and loyalty.

The killing of Höskuld, a kind and peaceful man, has shattered Flosi's belief in the goodness of humankind. The death has brought him much grief and anger, and he feels especially sorry for Njal, Höskuld's foster father, whom he has always respected for being one of the best lawyers in Iceland. Njal was very fond of Höskuld, and Flosi suspects that he loved him more than his biological sons. He remembers how delighted he was when, on behalf of Höskuld, Njal had asked for Hildigun's hand in marriage. And now Höskuld is dead.

It did not come as a surprise to Flosi when he was told that a lawsuit had been started over the slaying. He made no comment but realized he could not remain passive – as Hildigun's uncle, it was incumbent on him to do something to avenge the killing of his niece's husband. So, he sent word to his father-in-law, Hall of Sida, to Hall's son, Ljot, and to many other powerful men that they should come to the Althing with a large following. After that, he rode to Surt Asbjarnarson at Kirkjubaer and sent for Kolbein Egilsson, his brother's son, to come as well. Both promised to ride to the Althing to support him. From there, he rode to Höfdabrekka, the home of his friend Thorgrim the Showy, and asked him to ride to the Althing with him, too. Finally, he rode across Arnarstakk Heath and came to Solheimar, to visit his close friend Lödmund Ulfsson.

By the evening Flosi was exhausted, so he stayed overnight with Lödmund. The next morning, the two rode to Dal, where his friend Runolf Ulfsson lived. They received a warm welcome and were served a good meal. After the table had been cleared, Runolf finally asked: 'What brings you here?' Flosi answered: 'Alright. I trust you, Runolf, so I'll tell you my reason for coming. I want you to tell me the true story of the killing of Höskuld. You live close to where it took place, so you should know.' Runolf was direct with him and did not mince his words: 'Höskuld was slain, though he was completely innocent, and his death is mourned by everybody – but by no one more than Njal.' In response to Flosi's question about how matters stood now, Runolf told him that a panel of neighbours had been summoned and that notice of the slaying had already been given by Mörd Valgardsson. 'He's my kinsman, but he's not a good man. Only evil comes from him. But now, Flosi, give your wrath a rest and take the course which will lead to the least trouble, for Njal and other good men will make good offers. I'll ride with you to the Althing.'

Flosi is at the Althing, and he is pleased to see all his friends have kept their promise and that so many of his supporters are there. He is now summoned to the Law Council and asks the sons of Sigfus to walk with him. They come from the east towards the Law Council, while Njal and his sons walk from the west. Njal and two of his sons then take a seat. Only Skarphedin goes to the middle bench and continues to stand, with his arms folded rigidly and his eyes fixed on Flosi, glaring at him. Flosi wonders why Skarphedin is acting this way, but then he remembers that Hildigun and several others have told him that Skarphedin is headstrong – he has not only a hot temper but also a sharp tongue. It makes Flosi feel uncomfortable, but it is not as if he can tell Skarphedin to sit down. So, Flosi goes to the Law Council where the silver is lying in a pile and takes his time to examine and count it. The amount is correct and the silver is pure. 'This is a large amount of good money and readily paid out, as I expected,' he says. He feels relieved that blood vengeance has been avoided and that it has been possible to reach a settlement in a peaceful manner.

But just as he is about to gather the silver, Flosi notices a robe and a pair of boots lying next to the pile. He ignores the boots but picks up the robe and examines it. It is knee-length and sleeved. It has decorative borders and embroideries with fine gold and silver thread. A precious bead, instead of a button, is used to close the opening at the neck. He realizes that the robe is made of silk and probably very expensive. It must either have been imported or been part of someone's loot on a Viking expedition. He does not understand why it is there and wonders if it is intended as a gift or as a type of extra compensation. At first he is tempted to try it on, but he is taken aback by the feminine nature of the garment. So instead, Flosi asks the people at the Law Council who has given it. No one says a word. He is perplexed, laughs and then waves the robe a second time and asks again, who has given the robe, but still no one answers. He studies the faces of the men in the crowd, searching for a sign from at least one of them. Some of the men respond by nervously shaking their heads and avoid making eye contact with Flosi, but most just maintain their poker-faces and say nothing. By now, Flosi feels utterly confused. In his frustration, he asks yet again: 'Will no one dare tell me who gave the robe?' After another long silence, Skarphedin finally grins and replies with his own question: 'Flosi, who do you think might have given it?'

Since it was Skarphedin who replied, Flosi now suspects that the robe may actually be an insult. He has a flashback to his last visit with Hildigun, immediately after his meeting with Runolf. He had ridden straight from Dal to Ossabaer to check on Hildigun because he was concerned about her wellbeing after the sudden death of her husband. When he arrived, he could tell that his visit was expected and that she and her household had gone out of their way to give him a stately welcome. Upon entering the house, he was asked to sit in the cushioned high seat in the main room, but Flosi quickly realized that this was meant only to mock him for not taking action against Höskuld's murder. When Hildigun finally entered the room, Flosi said, 'I'm neither a king nor an earl, so there is no need to fix up the high seat for me.' Then, as he tossed off the cushions with a sweep of his hand, he said, 'Don't you dare make fun of me!'

Now, standing before the Law Council, in his mind he can still hear her short, chilly laugh in response. Back then, at her farm, he knew that she – a fierce and cold-hearted woman – had more insults in store for him. After he had been served a delicious meal by Hildigun's servants, she came back into the room, swept the hair away from her eyes and cried. He expressed his sincere condolences for her loss but could not help noticing that she was quick to wipe away her insincere tears. She then went to another room, opened a chest, took out her husband's bloodstained cloak, placed herself in front of Flosi and threw the cloak over his shoulders, clearly exposing the large stains of clotted blood which fell on both sides of him. 'Flosi,' she said, 'you gave this cloak to Höskuld as a gift, and now I give it back to you. He was slain in it. And now I charge you in the name of God and all good men, by the powers of your Christ and by your courage and manliness to avenge all the wounds which he received in dying. If you don't, you'll be an object of contempt to all men.'

Flosi could not believe her words. Never before had his manliness been challenged. He flung off the cloak and threw it back at her. As he stormed out of the house, he yelled: 'You're a monster! You want us to take blood vengeance, but that would be the worst for us all. Cold is the counsel of women.' He could not remember ever being so angry, for he knows he is a strong and masculine-looking man. He has fathered a son. Nonetheless, Hildigun's insinuation that he might be an unmanly man has been on his mind ever since.

In the mind of Viking Age and medieval Icelanders, cowardice and effeminacy were two aspects of the same thing. Nothing hit a man harder than the allegation that he was no man. Such affronts to honour are denoted by the Old Norse-Icelandic word 'nid'. It is difficult to define the word, but accusation with sexual import forms the core of the meaning.

Before answering Skarphedin, Flosi pauses to collect his thoughts. Finally, he clears his throat and exclaims, 'If you really want to know, then I'll tell you what I think. I believe that Old Beardless, your father, Njal, gave the robe, for there are many people who can't tell by his appearance whether he's a man or a woman.' Flosi immediately regrets his words, for he does not mean to insult Njal – but he is too angry to contain himself. He knows he has hit a sensitive nerve. People gossip about Njal's inability to grow a beard. Some even refer to his sons as 'dungbeardlins', implying they put dung in their mouths to grow their beards.

He is not surprised when Skarphedin, never at a loss for words, quickly stands up for his father. 'Don't you dare make slurs about him in his old age. You can tell that he's a man because he's had sons with his wife. And few of our kinsmen have been buried without taking vengeance for them.' To make matters worse, Skarphedin walks up to Flosi, picks up the robe and throws a pair of black trousers at him. 'You have more need of these,' Skarphedin says with a laugh. Flosi, now even more confused, asks why he might need the black trousers more than the silk cloak. Again, Skarphedin is quick to reply: 'Because if you are the sweetheart of the troll at Svinafell, as people say, he uses you as a woman every ninth night.'

Flosi flies into a rage. He has been openly accused of homosexuality, which everyone knows is considered a sin in Iceland. He angrily pushes the settlement money away, declaring that he will not take any of the silver and throwing both the black trousers and the boots at Skarphedin. He is now left with only two choices: either there will be no redress at all for Höskuld, or he and his men will take blood vengeance. Flosi announces, 'I'll neither offer nor accept peace.' He turns to the sons of Sigfus and tells them: 'Let's now go home. We'll all share the same fate.'

The conversation between Flosi and Skarphedin did mark the end of peace between the families. Judicial negotiations were swept away and armed conflict was soon inevitable. The vengeance was later accomplished in an attack by fire, in which Njal and his family perished.

8TH HOUR OF THE DAY
(13.00–14.00)

A CHIEFTAIN RETURNS
FROM A VIKING RAID

Svein Asleifarson and his crew have arrived at his home on Gairsay, one of the seventy or so islands in the Orkney archipelago off the northern coast of Scotland. His crew members have dropped anchor. Now some are busy attaching his ships to the dock with long, heavy ropes, while others sort through their armour – swords, spears, axes, bows and arrows, helmets and shields – all of which lie in a pile in the middle of each of the ships. A final group gathers the rich booty acquired during their latest trip to pillage and plunder. All the crew members are eager to carry the whole lot off the ships and onto the shore, where their friends and loved ones await them.

Svein is a wealthy and successful farmer, but twice a year

he sails abroad to harry. He does not need the extra income from these raids, but Viking blood runs in his veins and he always enjoys the adventure, even though each journey puts his life and those of his men at risk. In the spring, he leaves Orkney on what the calls his 'spring trip', starting out after he has sown seeds on his farm. He does not return home until his corn and grains have been harvested and safely stored away. He then leaves again in the early autumn on what he calls his 'autumn trip', and he does not come back until the first month of winter has ended. Typically, he raids in the Hebrides, an archipelago off the west coast of the Scottish mainland; in Caithness, a nearby county in the far north of Scotland; and in Ireland. One time he sailed all the way to the Scilly Isles, a cluster of islands off the south-western tip of England, from which he brought back a great deal of loot.

Svein spends the rest of each winter on Gairsay, where he entertains up to eighty men at his own expense in his enormously large hall built for that purpose. Despite his successes over the years as a Viking, Svein has finally decided that the upcoming autumn trip will be his last expedition.

During the past winter, he invited Harald Maddadarson, Earl of Orkney, to his farm for a magnificent feast in honour of his friend. During the gathering, Earl Harald recommended to Svein that he abandon the Viking profession, warning him that many Vikings eventually end up being killed during these raids. Though reluctant to agree with the earl at first, Svein soon began to realize that his friend's words were true and that he, too, had known many who had not returned alive. Svein even acknowledged to his friend that he was beginning to feel his age and was no longer as agile and quick with weapons as he once was. He promised to follow Earl Harald's advice: he would give up raiding forever after his next autumn trip.

Svein has a considerable fleet. Sometimes he sails off from the Orkney Islands with five, six or even seven ships on his plundering trips. On this last adventure with the fleet there are five large ships, all traditional warships built for speed and manoeuvrability – slender, with oar holes in a continuous line along the length of a ship, a mast that can be lowered and a shield batten on the outer side of the top strake, the line of planking that runs from the stem to the stern of a ship. These ships are perfect for raiding because of their ability to make surprise attacks. Once the crew has taken down the sails and lowered the mast, they can quietly row and sneak into a bay or fjord without being noticed – a tactic that Svein and his men have used many times.

As the fleet arrives home, Svein can see that a large crowd of people has gathered on the shore to greet them. Some have brought refreshments – milk, water, baked goods, even smoked meat – for the hungry and thirsty crew, who have been without fresh food for some weeks. Several people on the shore are his farmhands, who have come to help carry Svein's portion of the loot home to his farm. In the crowd, he recognizes his wife, Ingirid, and their two sons, Olaf and Andres. Many others are

A WOODCUT OF A NORSE SHIP LIKE THOSE THAT WOULD HAVE
SAILED IN SVEIN'S FLEET.

family members of his crew. But the crowd is larger than usual, mostly people who are curious to see what Svein and his crew have brought back. They were no doubt attracted by the ships' sails, as they are much more colourful than the ones he had when he left a few months ago.

Having found his sword, helmet and shield, Svein now disembarks along with Hakon, Earl Harald's son, whom he is fostering.

Fostering a child in the Nordic islands was common in the Middle Ages. It was regarded as a source of honour to the birth father. Usually, the fostering party was of a lower social status than the biological father. Original family ties and rights of inheritance were not affected, and it was not required for the fostered child's father to be deceased.

When Hakon came of age, Svein started taking him on Viking expeditions to build up Earl Harald's power. Ingirid and their sons now greet them both warmly. He can tell that Ingirid is relieved to have him back, though she has seen him depart and arrive so many times he thought she had stopped worrying about his safety when he goes raiding. Although she must know that he has a lot of blood on his hands, he has never told her about his many killings over the years. He suspects she would rather not know.

Svein's foreman, to whom he always entrusts the running of the farm when he is gone for long stretches of time, walks up to greet him. Svein is much indebted to him. He knows that whenever he goes raiding, it is a drain on the farm's manpower and means extra work for the foreman, who now wants to hear about his employer's latest adventure, especially the reason for the colourful sails. Although Svein is exhausted and badly wants to walk home to rest and be with his family, he briefs the foreman on the raid. He reports that on the first day, they sailed to the Hebrides, where they had no success because, he thinks, the islands had been raided so many times that either the inhabitants had little or nothing left, or they had hidden all their valuables, especially their precious metals, in the ground. 'We didn't consider it worth our time to dig in the ground looking for hoards,' Svein says. From the Hebrides, they had sailed down to the Isle of Man, but it was the same story there. 'We targeted some churches and monasteries, but they were completely empty. I was worried that our expedition would be a failure but decided to continue to Ireland, where fortunately we found some valuable loot.'

Then, on their way towards Dublin, good fortune struck as they met two merchant ships en route from England. Svein suspected they must be carrying goods to sell and probably had other valuables on board, so he ordered his men to sail close to the merchant ships. Once there, he directed his ships to line up, asked his men to rope them together side by side and directly face the English ships. He instructed his men to shoot arrows at the English to signal that they were going to attack, and then some of Svein's men jumped onto the English ships with their swords and spears and started hand-to-hand combat with their crews, who offered little resistance.

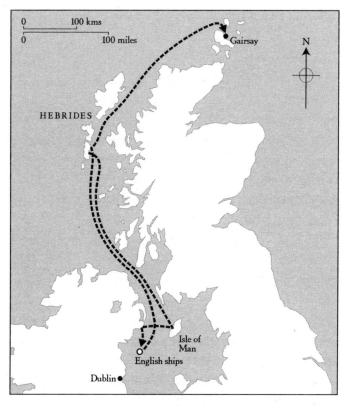

A MAP SHOWING THE JOURNEY SVEIN'S FLEET TOOK UNTIL THEY LOOTED
ENGLISH SHIPS AND TURNED BACK TOWARDS HOME.

The English crew members were tied to benches or the masts, with their hands behind their backs. Svein's crew ransacked the ships for booty, where they found lots of fine English broadcloth – a dense, plain woven cloth made of wool – as well as barrels of wine and mead. They robbed the English of every penny they had, leaving them only with some food and water and the clothes on their backs. 'After so much luck, I saw no point in continuing to Dublin,' Svein says. 'I decided to set course for the Hebrides to divide the loot with my crew. While we were in harbour there and before we set sail home to Gairsay, we decided to make a great show of our accomplishments and sail back home in style. We set up some of the English broadcloth as our awnings and stitched some of the cloth to the front of the sails, so they would seem to be woven of the most precious fabrics. We were quite a sight. Whenever we sailed close to shore, people stared at us. Those sails made us stand out,' he says with a laugh. 'So, we decided to call our expedition "The broadcloth Viking trip".'

By now, most of the crew members have disembarked. The British broadcloth, including the cloth that had been stitched onto the sails, is lying in a pile on the shore. Svein tells the people to take whatever they want, as he and his crew do not want any for themselves. Although the cloth is precious and probably intended for dignitaries, such as kings, princes, bishops and priests, they know it is not suitable for outdoor work. Svein looks at the people – mostly women – digging through and examining the cloth and shakes his head. 'Women,' he thinks to himself. 'Why is it that they can never seem to get enough of fineries?' He even sees Ingirid among them and feels a little embarrassed. It is not as if she is lacking anything, because over the years he has brought home many treasures for her. He consoles himself with the fact that she does not yet know that in the loot this time there is a festoon of beautiful glass beads which he intends to give to her when he can finally lie down with her at the end of this very long day.

The silver pennies robbed from the English have been brought to him in the buckets used for bailing. He asks the crew members to assemble so he can portion it out and pay them for their help and labour. In the past, he has sometimes used a scale, but this time there is so much silver he does not bother to weigh it. Each crew member brings his pouch and, digging into the bucket with his hand, Svein manages to fill each one while their wives eagerly watch on. From the expressions on all their faces, he knows they are all pleased with the trip's wages. Svein has also saved more than a handful of silver for his grateful foreman and, of course, he has kept plenty for himself.

People start to drift off now, with their English cloth and silver. Svein can see, too, that his crew members, now that they have been paid, are eager to leave and go home to their families. Soon, only a handful of his farmhands, as well as Ingirid, their two sons and Hakon, are left on the shore. Svein instructs one of his farmhands to keep close watch of the English wine and mead and tells the others to go back to his farm and cart a couple of horses so the beverages can be transported back home. Svein does not want to share these drinks with others. As a chieftain, he has obligations to host feasts several times during the year and he knows that Yule, the midwinter solstice feast to celebrate the longest night of the year and the beginning of more daylight time, will be coming soon, and guests often stay around for as long as twelve days to eat and drink at his farm. No too long after that will be the sacrifice to the winter god, Thorri, when again he will need to host a large number of people at a time when farmers and their families are often low on food and will want to eat and drink a lot.

'No slave woman this time?' asks Ingirid, as the five of them walk back to the farm. She is carrying some of the broadcloth she has picked out. He is pretty sure she is joking, but still he feels that she deserves an answer. 'No,' Svein says. 'We never made it to Dublin.' Ingirid says nothing, but Svein can hear their sons, who are walking behind them, chuckling. He suspects they overheard an argument between him and Ingirid a couple of years ago after he brought home a young slave woman from Ireland. At the time, he claimed it was to give Ingirid and her female servants an extra hand around the house. As it turned out, the woman was not a good worker and never bothered to learn the Norse language. Ingirid later accused him of having bought her simply for her good looks. To end the argument and relieve tensions in their marriage, he promised to marry the slave woman off to one of his farmhands. Ingirid still does not know that he gave the two a little plot of land to farm on.

As they approach the farmhouse, Svein can see the farm has been well tended to during his absence. He also smells the aroma of delicious food and can tell that Ingirid has gone out of her way to give him a warm welcome. He enters the longhouse and sees the servants busy preparing his favourite meals. 'It's good to be back home,' he says to Ingirid. 'Only one more expedition in the autumn, and then I'll be home for good.'

The next expedition would be the last expedition for Svein, but it did not end as he planned. He was killed in Dublin during his autumn trip. He and his men had armed themselves and walked to town as far as the gate, but this time the Dubliners were waiting for them and had formed an armed crowd to protect the city. Svein and his men, suspecting nothing, fell right into their trap. Once the raiders were inside, the Dubliners barred the gate and attacked. Svein and his men had no chance.

9TH HOUR OF THE DAY

(14.00–15.00)

A MAN FIGHTS IN A SINGLE COMBAT

K ormak Ögmundarson has arrived at Leidholm in Middalir, Iceland, where the duel between him and Bersi Veleifsson, nicknamed Duel-Bersi, is to take place. Kormak has a habit of running late, but on this occasion he is early. He now sits by himself on a knoll behind the site of the duel. His mother, Dalla, had not liked the idea of her son fighting in single combat, especially against Bersi, because she fears that he may be mortally wounded. Like everyone else, she knows that Bersi is a great warrior. His scarred face and body show that he has been in many fights. His weapons are exceptionally good for combat, including a sword named Hviting, which is razor sharp, bears a healing stone and has served Bersi well in many dangerous situations. When Dalla asked her son what sort of weapon he planned to use to withstand Hviting, Kormak replied, 'Just a large, sharp axe like the ones many men in Iceland own.'

His is actually a bearded axe, named because the lower bladed portion of the axe head extends further down than the butt, resembling a beard. It is a useful household tool for cutting branches or wood, but it can also be a handy weapon. Wielded properly, the beard on the axe can catch and disable an opponent's weapon or shield in combat. But the choice of an axe in the duel did not please his mother, who requested

A VIKING WAR AXE MADE FROM IRON.

Kormak ride to Reykir and ask Skeggi Skinna-Bjarnarson, a good friend who often gives her sound advice, if he could borrow his sword, Sköfnung. Kormak did as she said, but Skeggi, who had been quite grumpy that day, was not willing to let him have the sword, claiming that Sköfnung was slow while Kormak was headstrong and rash in his actions.

But Dalla was also headstrong and did not give up easily. When she heard back from Kormak, she was not discouraged because she knew that it often takes Skeggi time to make up his mind. So, a few days later, she sent Kormak off once again to ask for Sköfnung. This time, Skeggi was in a better mood and finally agreed to lend his sword to Kormak – but it could only be used under certain conditions, he warned, or the sword would be too difficult for him to manage. First, a pouch went with the sword, which he was directed to leave alone. Next, Kormak was told not to let the sun shine on the upper boss of the sword hilt. Also, he should not wield the sword until he was getting ready for combat. Finally, Kormak should sit by himself when he got to the battlefield, hold the sword blade in front of him and blow on it.

If he followed these instructions, he would see a little snake crawl out from under the boss. Then Kormak should turn the sword sideways to make it possible for the snake to crawl back under the boss again. Kormak found these instructions very bizarre, but he took the sword, rode home to his mother and tried to draw the sword to show it to her. When he pulled at the sword, however, a strange thing happened. It would not budge from the scabbard, no matter how hard he tried. In his frustration, Kormak placed his feet against the hilt to get some leverage when he pulled, but still the sword would not release. Kormak's efforts only tore off the pouch, which Skeggi had said to leave alone. Sköfnung the sword howled in response.

Today, Kormak follows Skeggi's instructions to sit by himself and does not engage with the fifteen men he has taken with him as required by the terms of a duel. As he waits for his appointed meeting with Bersi, he uses the time to process what is about to happen. He knows that he is not a warrior, that he has had little training in how to wield weapons and that he is not physically strong. He comes from relatively high birth, so he has never had to do much farm work because there have always been enough farmhands to do the bulk of the labour. He does not mind farm work and helps now and then, but he is more of an intellectual than a farmer and has always preferred to spend his time composing poetry. He has a reputation for being a good skald, though some people do not appreciate his love poems about Steingerd Thorkelsdottir, who is now married to Bersi.

To pass the time and distract himself from his upcoming battle, Kormak begins to examine Sköfnung more carefully. Though he does not know much about weapons, he can tell that it is a high-quality sword. It is designed to be used one-handed, like most swords, but this one has a double-sided blade. The hand grip is wood-fitted around the tang of the blade, and the sword has a copper alloy inlay with an ornate design on the pommel and cross guard. The scabbard is made from leather-covered wood, lined on the inside with wool. The sword is clearly a treasure. He wonders if Skeggi, his father or his grandfather had acquired it from central Europe, where the swords are manufactured using crucible steel, making them much stronger than most locally made swords, which often have brittle blades and are prone to break in battle.

Duels were typically held on an island, as implied by 'holmganga' (island-going), the Old Norse-Icelandic name for duel. Occasions for duel include the breakdown of court proceedings or a court judgement unacceptable to one party.

While handling Sköfnung, Kormak carelessly forgets the instructions Skeggi gave him about using the sword. Earlier, he had girt himself with the sword exposed outside his clothes. He does not notice the sun shining on the boss of Sköfnung's hilt. Now, when he reaches to draw the sword, he cannot do so and clumsily steps on the boss. The little snake comes howling out of the scabbard. Kormak freezes in fear – he realizes the spell of the sword has been broken just as he is about to start his duel.

As he ponders his fate, Kormak notices a man preparing the place for the duel.

Acting according to the prescribed laws, the man places two cloaks, or tarses, on the ground, each measuring five ells square (a Viking ell was about 18 inches), with loops at the corners to be secured by pegs. As the man prepares the tarses, Kormak can see him grasping his ear lobes and can faintly hear him utter an invocation. The man marks out three spaces around the cloak, each space a foot in length. Finally, and outside these marked spaces, he installs posts called hazel poles and runs four strings from pole to pole to create a stretch of ground within which the duel is to take place. If someone steps with just one foot outside the hazel poles, he is said to be retreating. If he steps out with both feet, he is said to be running.

Each combatant has three shields to begin the fighting, and each has an assistant to hold the extra shields until they are needed. He who is challenged to the duel has the right to strike first. When the shields are used up, a combatant can only protect himself with his weapon, and only while standing on the cloak. If one is wounded such that blood falls onto the cloak, there is no longer any obligation to continue fighting. In the end, the one who is the more wounded is to release himself by paying a duel ransom of three marks of silver.

Kormak is the one who had challenged Bersi to today's duel because he detests Bersi for taking Steingerd as his wife, the woman Kormak still loves and thought he would marry. Kormak remembers the first time he saw her. A whale had come ashore onto Vatnsnes, which was the property of his mother's family. He had been offered the choice of going to the mountains to look for sheep, or of going to the shore to process the whale. Kormak had chosen to go to the mountains together with Tosti, an overseer whose job it is to arrange for sheep searches. They had eventually arrived not very far away at Gnupsdale to spend the night there, when down the hall he had seen the feet of a woman sticking out between the threshold and the bottom of the door. Kormak had never seen such beautiful feet, and he immediately became smitten with the woman.

A little later, when he entered the hall, he overheard two women talking about his looks. One, whom he suspected was a slave woman, said he was dark and ugly, and his eyes were too black. The other woman, whom he later learned was called Steingerd and whose feet he had so admired, was more complimentary. She said she found him handsome in every respect, with the exception of his hair, which was curled on his forehead. When he heard this, Kormak became very self-conscious of his hair. The next morning, when he saw her combing her own long and beautiful hair, he walked over to her and asked to borrow her comb. When she gracefully agreed, he realized there was a mutual affection and attraction between them.

After he and Tosti returned from the mountains, Kormak

rode home to his mother and asked her to make him some fine clothes so he might appear more attractive to Steingerd the next time he visited her. His mother reluctantly agreed and warned him that Steingerd's father might not approve of their relationship. From then on, Kormak made frequent visits to Gnupsdale, where Steingerd was being fostered. Sadly, Kormak was to find out that his mother was right. When Steingerd's father, Thorkel, discovered their affair, he was displeased and brought Steingerd back home to Tunga. That did not stop Kormak, however. He continued to visit Steingerd there, which only irritated Thorkel even more.

In the meantime, Thorkel had become friendly with the two boisterous sons of Thorveig the Sorceress, a woman skilled in magic, who lived at Steinsstadir in Midfjord. Thorkel had come to despise Kormak so much that he incited her sons to ambush Kormak and kill him. So, one day when Kormak came to visit Steingerd, the two brothers attacked him. It was a vicious fight that went on and on until even Thorkel eventually entered the fray. Kormak might not have survived the one-sided battle if Steingerd had not run out and seized her father's weapons. In the end, Kormak managed to kill both of Thorveig's sons and was not seriously wounded himself. After the attack, Kormak went to see Thorveig to direct her to move away from the district and tell her he would not pay compensation for the deaths of her sons. In return, Thorveig cast a spell on him so he would never enjoy Steingerd's love.

When next Kormak visited Steingerd, she asked him to seek her father's friendship and request her hand in marriage. But after the betrothal and wedding date were arranged, his feelings for Steingerd and the whole arrangement strangely began to cool, so much so that he forgot the date of the wedding and did not show up – realizing too late that he was under Thorveig's spell. Thorkel and his sons were greatly offended by Kormak's breach of promise and soon approached Bersi, a good friend of theirs, whose wife had died. Bersi asked for Steingerd's hand and received a positive answer from the male members of her family. When Kormak heard the news, he rode to Bersi's farm with the intention of snatching Steingerd and taking her home with him, but Bersi flatly refused to let her go. Instead, he offered his unappealing sister in marriage as compensation – a huge insult. It was then that Kormak challenged Bersi to a duel.

Kormak takes a deep breath and joins his men. It is a cool summer day, but he is sweating, and his hands feel so clammy he worries he may not be able to get a good grip on Sköfnung. Bersi and his followers finally arrive, as have many other people to see their encounter.

Bersi has the right to strike first and splits Kormak's shield in half. Kormak strikes back and destroys Bersi's shield. Before long, all six shields have been rendered useless. The spectators are upset to see the shields go to waste, but they know the

A RECONSTRUCTION OF A VIKING AGE SHIELD, MADE
FROM WOOD AND IRON.

shields are not that fine – made of inexpensive wood and
not decorated. The fight goes on. Kormak strikes at Bersi but
misses his target. When Bersi strikes back with his sword,
Sköfnung crashes into it. It knocks the point off Hviting in
front of the ridge along the middle of the blade. A hole is
nicked in Sköfnung as well.

Bersi's sword point falls onto Kormak's hand, leaving a
scratch on his thumb. Even though the scratch is not deep,
blood drips onto the cloak. Kormak badly wants to continue

fighting but the people intercede, insisting that he and Bersi must stop because blood has touched the cloak. Kormak is annoyed and cannot help pointing out to the crowd that Bersi has not gained a great victory from this little mishap. Bersi is quick to claim the duel ransom, and Kormak promises that the money will be paid to him, so they part on these terms. Kormak is not pleased, however, and rides home to his mother, who bandages his hand, which is now quite swollen. In the meantime, Kormak's friends try to sharpen the nick in Sköfnung, Skeggi's special sword. The more the sword is sharpened, however, the larger the nick becomes.

Kormak later learned that Steingerd had divorced
Bersi and married another man, a peaceful man whom
Kormak came to despise as much as he despised Bersi.
Kormak ended his life harrying in the British Isles
and died of wounds sustained in Scotland.

10TH HOUR OF THE DAY
(15.00–16.00)

A WOMAN DECIDES TO DIVORCE HER HUSBAND

Unn Mardardottir has arrived at the Althing, but the ride this year was different. She is not with her husband, Hrut Herjolfsson, like last year, as he claimed he was busy travelling to the West Fjords. For this trip, she has been accompanied by Sigmund Özurarson, a kinsman of her husband, who rode with her all the way from Hrutsstadir to Thingvellir. Sigmund had been reluctant to ride with Unn at first, agreeing to it only under two conditions: that she ride back with him and that there be no hidden plot against him or her husband. Unn agreed to those terms; she desperately needed to speak with her father, Mörd Sighvatsson.

Once Sigmund confirmed he would take her, Unn sent word to her father, who invited her to stay with him in his booth. She looks forward to reconnecting with him, as she has not seen him for a while. She knows she will appreciate all the delicacies and gifts that he always gives her, but this year she needs his help and advice even more.

Once she and Sigmund arrive, he takes off to be with his relatives. Unn starts out on her own to find her father's booth. When she sees it off in the distance, the tears she has been holding back since the trip began finally burst out. She tethers her horse and runs to the lake to splash cold water on her face to hide her red, swollen eyes. She does not want her father to see that she has been crying.

When Unn meets her father in his booth, he embraces her. She is comforted by the warmth of his body and the strength of his arms. Clearly, he does not sense that anything is wrong. He invites her to sit down on one of the sheep skins on the ground, then puts a blanket over her shoulders. Although it is early summer, Unn is chilled to the bone. She had dressed in her finest clothes to look beautiful for her father, but they are too sheer to keep her warm. Unn is warmed too, when her father gives her some of her favourite foods, which he had brought with him from home. 'How kind of you,' she says to him. The first taste of her mother's cooking makes her feel so homesick she struggles to hold back her tears. Her father says nothing, just sits back to look at his daughter as she eats. Although she is looking down and pretending to focus on her food, she can sense he is studying her.

Soon, he gently tucks his hand under her chin to lift her face. 'Look at me, my beautiful daughter,' he says, 'and tell me how your husband, Hrut, is doing.' Unn swallows hard and tries to compose herself. She takes what feels like a whole minute to think before she responds. 'I can only say good things about Hrut in the matters over which he has control.' She can tell by the puzzled look on his face that her father is not satisfied with her answer, but he does not say anything. During the entire ride to Thingvellir, she has rehearsed what she will tell her father, but now words fail her. She is not afraid of him. That is not it. He has always been a good and supportive father to her. She just cannot get the words out, at least not yet. Everything seems too real, too hard to express.

She truly meant what she said about Hrut. She knows that in his youth, he was a successful Viking, managing to bring back much booty whenever he raided. She also knows he is held in high esteem at the Norwegian court, where he spent several years with King Harald Greycloak, son of Eirik Bloodaxe. The king's mother, Gunnhild Özurardóttir, had become very fond of Hrut, too. Hrut is quite wealthy; she does not lack for anything. Whenever she asks for new clothes or jewellery for herself, or for more food for the household, Hrut never says no. After they got married, he had placed in her hands full authority over all matters inside their house.

Yet she had not been pleased when she learned that her father had decided to marry her off to Hrut. She could not put her finger on what it was, but there was something unappealing about Hrut. She tried not to show it, but she had felt depressed at their wedding when he hardly looked at her. And their wedding night had been a disaster. She expected that they would be intimate, but Hrut had just rolled onto his side and away from her in their bed, leaving her wondering what was on his mind, what was wrong.

Eventually, her father asks, 'What's bothering you, Unn? You were sad when I saw you at the Althing last year, but this year you seem even sadder. I know that you don't like living out there at Hrutsstadir, but I have encouraged you to be content with your lot after I married you off to a wealthy and influential man.' Unn does not know what to say. She just shakes her head. 'Well,' her father says, 'I can tell that you don't want anyone else to know about this, so tell me what it is. You know that you can count on me to help you, whatever the problem is.'

At this point, Unn cannot hold back her tears. Her father wraps his arms around her again and strokes her long hair while she sobs. When she finally stops, he says, 'Let's go where no one can hear us.' Unn expresses her gratitude, for other booths are very close to her father's. She does not want anyone to overhear what she is about to tell him.

The two find a private spot not far from the assembly site. They sit on a lava rock overgrown with soft, comfortable moss. Her father has brought along his blanket and places it over her shoulders. 'It's becoming clearer to me that things cannot be good between you and Hrut,' her father says. 'Whether the problem is big or small in your eyes, I need to know what is bothering you or I cannot be of any help.' Unn takes a deep breath. She has never felt comfortable talking to her father about sexual matters, so she thinks, *how can I tell him about this?*

But she knows she cannot wait any longer. She has taken up enough of her father's time. She has kept him far too long from his important work at the Althing. She must tell him now. 'Alright,' she says. 'I'll tell you.' But she looks away from her father. She does not want to see the expression on his face when he hears what she is about to tell him. 'I want to divorce Hrut and this is why: we've never been able to have sexual intercourse in a way that gives me pleasure.' Unn is relieved that she has finally revealed this much to her father, but she knows there is more to tell. She can only guess that this must have come as a surprise, even a shock, to him, that he assumed there would be other reasons for divorce – physical or verbal abuse, excessive frugality or infidelity – but not this. Her father stares at her, then says, 'How is this possible? I need more details.' Unn begins to feel more comfortable. She knows her father is a good listener, is not judgmental and does not jump to conclusions, so she decides to tell him the full story.

'When we're in bed at night and he rolls over to touch me and try to be intimate with me, he cannot penetrate, so I get no satisfaction from him. We have both tried in every possible way to enjoy each other, but nothing works. The strange thing is that when we part, he shows that he's just like any other man.' Her father looks at her, then shakes his head in disbelief. 'I've never heard of such a thing,' he says. Then Unn confesses that she is actually terrified of Hrut. 'What if he were able to penetrate me?' she asks. 'Would he get stuck inside me, the way the dogs would get locked together when they were mating back on the farm? I'm afraid!' Again, her father shakes his head.

Unn can see he is confused, that he has no idea what she might be talking about. So she reminds him of the time when she was a little girl. She had found their two dogs by the barn, their behinds touching like they were tied together. In panic, she had run to the farmhouse to tell him and he had assured her that it was OK; they were just mating the way dogs mate. But when she went back, the dogs were still stuck together, so again she went back to tell her father. He sent one of his farmworkers out to pour cold water over the two dogs to separate them. 'I don't want that to happen to me,' Unn says. This time, her father stifles a laugh and says, 'Have no worries, my dear. This doesn't happen to humans.'

He gives her another warm hug. Then he calls her very brave for being so honest with him about such an intimate problem. 'Thank you for trusting in me,' he says. He thinks for a while and then adds, 'I have a plan, which will serve you well, but you must follow it exactly. If you deviate from it, it will not work.'

Her father directs Unn to ride back home with Sigmund now, not to wait until the Althing is over. 'I fully expect that Hrut will have returned from his trip and be there to greet you. You must be pleasant and compliant to him, so he thinks there has been a change in you for the better. Don't under any circumstances show coldness to him this summer, autumn or next winter. I know it's going to be hard for you, but you must do as I say.' Then her father says, 'When spring comes, you must pretend to be ill and take to your bed. Hrut will not try to find the cause of your illness. In fact, he will ask people to care for you as best they can. Then he will go to the West Fjords together with Sigmund to bring back his wares, so he'll be away for most of the summer.'

Her father asks Unn if she has any questions so far. When she says no, he continues, 'When people ride to the Althing next summer, get out of your bed and summon some men to travel with you, as though you want to go to the Althing, too. When you've done that, go back to your bed and with those men at your husband's bedside, name witnesses and declare yourself legally divorced from Hrut.'

Mörd explains to her that this is perfectly allowable under the rules of the Althing and the law of the land. 'But there's a little more to do. After that, you must repeat the naming of the witnesses at the homes of each of these men, and then ride away over Laxardale Heath as far as Holtavarda Heath, for you likely won't be pursued as far as Hrutafjord. You must keep riding until you come to me. At that point, I'll take over the lawsuit, and you'll never come into Hrut's hands again.'

Unn does not know what to say. She does not fully understand what her father has said, but she trusts him entirely, for she knows that he is a very wise man. 'I'll do what you say, father. I'm so very grateful to have your support and help. Thank you.' She puts her arms around him and gives him a kiss on both cheeks. 'I'll find Sigmund now to ride back to Hrutsstadir. Goodbye.'

Unn carefully followed her father's instructions and eventually managed to divorce Hrut. She did not know that when Hrut decided to leave Norway for Iceland and was gone for a while, he befriended Gunnhild, the king's mother, who had asked if he had a woman in Iceland he wanted to marry. Hrut had lied and said no, but clearly Gunnhild, who had become fond of Hrut, had had her suspicions. So she had cast a spell on him that he would never be able to have sexual pleasure with the woman he planned to marry. Hrut later married two other women, with whom he had sixteen sons and two daughters. Unn, too, remarried. Her husband was Valgard Jorundsson, with whom she had a son named Mörd Valgardsson.

A HOUSEWIFE PREPARES A SPECIAL DINNER

It is the first day of Thorri, the name of the fourth winter month, and true to custom in Iceland, Sigrid Steingrimsdottir and her husband Sigmund Arnason are getting ready to celebrate. In some parts of the country, it is the duty of the wife to welcome Thorri, but here in the eastern part of the island where Sigrid and Sigmund live, the task falls to the husband. Sigrid does not really know who or what Thorri is, and she doubts her husband has any clear idea either, but she has heard from her ancestors that Thorri is a sort of winter spirit or weather god and that he has a winter spirit wife or daughter, Goa, which is also the name of the fifth winter month. Sigrid is clear about one thing, though: on the first day of Thorri, she is expected to treat her husband exceptionally well. In fact, some people call the first day of Thorri Husband's Day.

Even while it was still dark this morning, Sigmund got up very early to go outside into the cold and the snow with only his shirt and under-breeches – not even his shoes – to greet and invite Thorri into their house. Sigrid has never asked him what he does outside on the first day of Thorri, but she has heard rumours from others that the man of the house puts on his shirt and then places only one foot through his under-breeches, which then sag down around his ankle. He then hops on the other foot all around the exterior of the farmhouse, still dragging his underpants with the one foot, before he finally ushers Thorri in. Sigrid has no idea if the mysterious Thorri is in their house yet – if he is, he is invisible – but she knows that she must treat her husband well, exceptionally well.

After checking on their two sons, who were both fast asleep, she got up, dressed and kindled the cooking fire. By the time her chilled husband came in from the snow, she had prepared a very special breakfast, a meal typically reserved for the Yule celebration: barley porridge with honey and milk. She made sure Sigmund did not eat all of it – since she had gone to the trouble of making such a delicious morning meal, she thought some of it should be preserved for the children when they woke up. Besides, she would like a taste of the porridge herself. She could tell by the look on Sigmund's face that he was pleased with her efforts. She flashed a satisfied look back after she noticed that he had taken his time to eat and scrape his bowl clean with his wooden spoon. He even gave her a kiss on the cheek after he had finished.

It is now late afternoon and Sigrid finds herself very busy. Sigmund has invited neighbours to their house for the celebration called *Thorrablot* (sacrifice to Thorri), and they will be arriving soon. She knows her neighbours do not expect anything fancy – just traditional Icelandic food that is eaten throughout the winter. It is not an easy time of the year to host dinner, however. Food is scarce for everyone, and most families live on whatever they have managed to preserve from the summer and autumn harvests. But Sigrid has prepared well, not only stocking up on food and preserving it but also rationing their food supplies.

A couple of days ago, Sigrid fetched a new supply of hard fish from their storage hut and placed it in a large bowl intended for the guests, but it has been difficult for her to keep her children's hands out of the bowl – they love dried fish, too, especially if it is smeared with butter. Sigrid and Sigmund are lucky to have plenty of hard fish, for they live close to the shore in the East Fjords, where the sea is teeming with cod, haddock and plaice. Sigmund often rows out in his boat to fish. When the catch has been good, Sigrid and Sigmund work together to dry the fish, which will prevent damage from bacteria, mould and insects. First, they gut the fish, then remove their heads and split the fish along their spines to make the drying time shorter, before hanging them on wooden racks to dry in the sun. But that is only part of the process. After the drying period, which can take quite some time, the fish have to be matured in airy conditions inside in their drying room.

On occasion, Sigmund and his neighbours find a beached whale, which they cut up and share. Sigrid always likes it when that happens because it means lots of extra meat. This year, however, they have already consumed most of their whale meat, because last summer the men only found one to butcher. Fortunately, Sigrid had taken some of the fibrous, fatty tissue from the underside of the whale and pickled it in sour milk whey, which she will serve at dinner today. She also salvaged some of the blubber, so her guests will be able to sample some of these tasty treats as well.

Luckily, during the year Sigmund also came home on occasion with Greenland sharks (*hakarl*). It is always his job to prepare them. He starts by cleaning the shark with seawater and removing the head and cartilage. Then he buries what is left in a pit dug close to the sea and covers it with stones, seaweed or turf. At high tide, the seawater floods over the carcass to ferment it and rid it of its ammonia odour. This fermentation can take weeks or months; the length of time depends on the temperature and the season during which the shark has been caught. Once the meat is soft and there is no longer any hint of ammonia, he digs it up, strings it and hangs it in their well-ventilated shed, where he leaves it to dry. This drying period, too, varies from weeks to months depending not only on the weather and the time of year but also on which parts of the shark have been saved.

Now, Sigrid sends Sigmund out to the drying shed to retrieve some chunks of shark. Even though it is Husband's Day, she assumes that it is not unreasonable to ask him to help, and he seems happy to comply. 'Cut the chunks into cubes and place them on a plate,' she says. Sigrid can see him in the shed, nibbling at a few pieces of the shark – *hakarl* is one of his favourite delicacies. She is not worried that there will not be enough for the guests, because there is plenty of it on hand.

Moreover, *hakarl* is an acquired taste. Not everyone likes it. Sigrid has told Sigmund many times that she would rather eat a worm than a piece of his cured shark. The taste of *hakarl* lingers in the mouth, and she can already smell Sigmund's bad breath. 'Don't expect any intimacies for a couple of days,' she says, 'and don't try to kiss me.' He laughs; it is the same story every time. When it comes to *hakarl*, Sigrid is mostly interested in the skin, which she uses for making shoes, though she is aware that in tough times some people even boil and eat the skin. She tends to throw out the shark's eggs, intestines and the cartilage or gristle, though poor people will eat these parts and use the thinly sliced fatty brown meat from the belly flaps as butter.

While Sigmund cuts the shark, Sigrid goes to their smoke house, a turf-roofed hut, to get *hangikjöt*, smoked lamb or mutton, which is hanging on hooks on rafters inside. Smoking the meat is Sigmund's job. Using mostly peat and dried manure as fuel, he funnels smoke up to the meat to half-cook it at a low temperature, high above the flames. Even though Sigrid and Sigmund keep the sheep mostly for their wool, they slaughter a few lambs or sheep every autumn for their meat. What they cannot eat fresh, they smoke for the winter months. *Hangikjöt* is everyone's favourite, so she takes down two whole legs of lamb and tells Sigmund to carve them into thin slices.

Like other women, Sigrid tries to use just about everything from a slaughtered sheep. Nothing is wasted, not even the head. To prepare what is called *svid*, she puts a stick through the nose of the sheep and then torches the skin and fleece of the head on an open fire. After that, she cleaves the head and removes the brain, then puts the head in cold salted water for a couple of days. When they do not have enough salt, she smokes the head instead. Earlier in the day, she made sure to heat a large batch of water, because the head needs to be boiled until the meat loosens from the bone. She checks now and can tell that the two half-heads are done, so she takes them out and puts them on a plate. She is pleased to see that the eyes and ears – both delicacies – are still there. She expects these will be kept for her sons as special treats, as the guests often go for the cheeks and tongue instead.

Sigrid then goes to the storage place next to the room used for cooking, where she has two vats of whey with fermented meat. In one, she keeps *hrutspungar*, pressed soured rams' testicles. She has been told they are very nutritious for pregnant women. She certainly consumed her own share when she was expecting their two sons and they turned out well, so it must be true, she thinks. The other vat contains *lundabaggar*, loin bags, which are made from the sirloin of sheep wrapped up with some suet in the colon and then sewn closed in the shape of sausages. They took her a long time to prepare, so she hopes they taste good and that the guests like them.

Sigrid takes the time now to count what she has gathered for dinner so far: hard fish, whale blubber, shark, smoked lamb, sheep's heads, rams' testicles and loin bags. She realizes she will also need lots of butter and is relieved to find she has plenty. She wonders if she should make flat bread but then notices the flour bin is almost empty. If she uses up what she has, she knows it will be expensive to replenish because most grains have to be imported. She consults with Sigmund, who says, 'Go for it! We're not paupers. Maybe a ship from Norway carrying grain will come soon. Let's impress our neighbours.' To this, Sigrid replies, 'Alright then, but you'll need to feed the cooking fire.'

Flatbread is easy to make. Sigrid puts flour, water and some salt into a bowl and kneads it together into a dough. When it is firm, she makes small balls and flattens them with her hands. She places them on a pan hanging over the cooking fire and regularly flips them, so they are baked on both sides. She is pleased that she is able to make twelve flatbreads without emptying her flour bin.

'I think we're finally done with the food,' Sigrid says to Sigmund, but then asks him: 'What about the seal's flippers?' 'Don't worry,' he says. 'Hardly anyone eats those any longer.' He looks around and nods approvingly. 'I married a good woman,' he says. Their sons stare at all the food and are eager to dive in, as they have had nothing to eat all day other than the leftover porridge from breakfast.

Sigrid looks around again and realizes she has been so preoccupied with food preparations that she has not had time to think about cleaning the house, never mind her own

THIS OVAL BROOCH (DATING FROM *C.*900–1000) WAS ORNAMENTAL AND
ORIGINALLY BRIGHTLY GILDED. IT WOULD HAVE BEEN WORN BY A
WOMAN TO FASTEN HER DRESS.

appearance. She instructs Sigmund to put some more peat
and wood on the long fire. In the meantime, she shakes the
dust out of the skins and woollen blankets covering the raised
platforms along the sides of the house and tells her sons to put
fresh straw and hay on the sunken, stamped-earth floor. She
quickly puts a clean woollen dress over her chemise, takes out
her little treasure chest and picks out her two best brooches,
which she pins to the front straps of her dress. Between the
two brooches she attaches a festoon of glass beads, a gift
from her husband when they were newly married. 'You look
beautiful,' Sigmund says.

The boys look out of the narrow peepholes in the house to see if the guests are arriving yet. They cannot see much, for even though Sigmund has opened the inside shutters, it is already dark outside. Sigmund and Sigrid go out to find their neighbours approaching with their children in tow. One of the women hands Sigrid some goat's cheese and one of the men gives Sigmund a jug of ale, which he has made from sprouted barley and water, fermented with yeast. Sigrid detests ale almost as much as she detests *hakarl*, but she likes the way ale always puts her husband in an exceptionally good mood. 'Come in,' Sigrid says. She knows it has been a long walk for them in the snow and they will enjoy all the food and the warmth from the long fire. Now she can finally sit back in the hope that Thorri will be pleased with their sacrifice and provide them with a good end to a long, cold winter.

12TH HOUR OF THE DAY
(17.00–18.00)

A MAN IS COMPENSATED FOR THE LOSS OF HIS BROTHER

Egil Skallagrimsson enters the hall of King Athelstan of England to find him drinking with his men amid much merriment and glee. Egil is not pleased but in a sad and ugly mood. Earlier, he suffered a terrible personal loss fighting alongside these same men, and he resents that they are cheerful and celebrating. He stands in the doorway, glaring at the king until he is seen waiting there. When the king finally takes notice, Egil squints back sternly through his piercing black eyes. The king quickly gives orders to clear the lower bench for

A WATERCOLOUR-ON-PAPER MANUSCRIPT ILLUMINATION
OF EGIL SKALLAGRIMSSON.

his men. He walks up to Egil, greets him and invites him to sit in the high seat which faces the king.

The history leading up to this tense moment goes back over two years, when Egil and his brother, Thorolf, decided they must leave Norway. The story goes that Egil had befriended a certain Ölvir, who worked for Thorir, one of King Eirik Bloodaxe's friends. Ölvir managed Thorir's farm and its farmhands. He also collected debts for Thorir and looked after his money. One day, Egil felt bored, so he asked Ölvir if he could come along on his next trip to collect debts. Ölvir said yes, there was room on the ship for Egil to join him and his men. Although it was quite cramped on the ship, Egil decided to take his weapons.

They set off, but soon the ship encountered rough weather, with strong unfavourable winds. Still, they sailed on, even rowing when they had to. When they finally landed at a place called Atloy Island early one evening, the crew was exhausted. From the shore they could see a large farm owned by King Eirik Bloodaxe and Queen Gunnhild. It was there that Ölvir, his men and Egil hoped to find a wholesome meal and comfortable beds for the night. But first the men had to haul the ship above the shoreline, then walk to the farm. When they arrived, they met a man called Bard, who ran the farm for the king and queen and served them well. Ölvir explained to Bard the purpose of their trip and asked if they could stay the night. Bard agreed, then led them to a fire room which was separated from the other buildings. He ordered a large fire made for his guests so they could dry their clothes. Once their clothes were ready, Bard returned with his servants, who laid a table for them, but the food was meagre: bread, butter and bowls of curds. Egil was surprised. 'Could this be all of it?' he thought. He was not happy, and he showed it. Bard noticed and began to apologize to the visitors. 'It's a shame there is no ale in the house to welcome you,' he said, 'but you must get by with what we have. I have plenty of mattresses, so lie down and get some sleep.'

Egil struggled to fall asleep. Just as he was finally drifting off, he was awakened by noises outside. He recognized the voices as those of King Eirik Bloodaxe and Queen Gunnhild. He could hear the king talking to one of Bard's farmhands. Bard had invited the royal couple to a feast, but the host was now nowhere to be found. 'Where is he?' Egil heard King Eirik ask. The man explained that Bard was serving guests, Thorir's men, in the fire room. The king gave orders to fetch Bard and invite his guests to the hall.

When Bard, Egil and Ölvir's men entered, the king welcomed Ölvir and offered him a place at the table opposite him in the high seat. Egil sat next to Ölvir. Lots of ale was served, and as the night wore on many of Ölvir's companions became very drunk, including Egil. Whenever Egil was given a horn of ale, he would immediately ask for another. He could see that this was irritating Bard, who eventually approached the queen. Egil watched as the two mixed something in his next drink and made a sign over it. When the serving woman handed it to Egil, he took out his knife, stabbed the palm of his hand, then carved runes on the horn and smeared them with his blood. The horn shattered and the drink spilled onto the straw on the floor. By this time, Ölvir was so drunk he did not notice. He was about to pass out, so Egil got up and led him over to the door. When they reached it, Bard hurried up to them with another full horn and asked Ölvir to drink a farewell toast. In a rage, Egil grabbed the horn and tossed it away. He quickly drew his sword and thrust it so deep into Bard's stomach that the point came out his back. Bard staggered, then fell down, dead, while Ölvir dropped to the floor, spewing vomit.

A VIKING AGE DRINKING HORN, KEPT AT THE
HISTORICAL MUSEUM IN NORWAY.

Egil fled and spent the night on the move. When dawn broke, he found himself on a promontory, from where he saw an island offshore. He gathered his helmet, sword and the head of his spear, wrapped the weapons in his cloak to make a bundle that he tied to his back, and swam to the island. Later that day, he saw a ship approaching, so he lay down in the shrub to hide. He saw nine men come ashore and split into search parties, leaving three men to guard the ship. When the parties disappeared behind a hill, Egil crept down to the waterfront, along the beach and onto the ship. The three onboard did not notice him until he was upon them. He killed two with a single blow, then chopped off the leg of the third, tossing them all overboard and taking off with the ship. He rowed and rowed all the way back to Thorir's farm, where he met up with his brother, Thorolf, and told him what had happened. Thorolf knew what this meant. 'We can no longer stay in Norway,' he said. 'We must leave as soon as possible.'

The two equipped a longship and took on a crew to go raiding in the Baltic and beyond. They fought and won many battles and pirated huge amounts of booty. While sailing near Saxony and Flanders, they heard that the King of England needed soldiers. Chances for booty were high, they were told, so they decided to join. King Athelstan welcomed them warmly and invited them to enter his service and help defend his country. Not long after, the king learned that King Olaf the Red of Scotland had gathered an army and entered his land. His chieftains and counsellors advised King Athelstan to start an army in the south of England and move northwards across the country to recruit more troops. The king appointed

Thorolf and Egil to lead the army that rallied there, as it was made up of forces that the Vikings had brought to the king.

King Athelstan sent messengers to King Olaf the Red: he wanted to challenge him to battle and proposed Wen Heath Forest as the site. The eventual battle was hard-fought, with many losses on both sides. Thorolf fought harder than anyone else. Egil last saw Thorolf carrying his standard as he led a force of soldiers around the side of the forest, from where he planned to make a surprise attack on the vulnerable side of King Olaf's men. Soon after, Egil heard the Scots let out a victory cry, and he feared the worst for his brother. When he saw one of Thorolf's soldiers withdraw with his standard, he knew Thorolf had been killed. He was told that Thorolf had charged ahead so fast that few of his men were still with him when the Scottish men counter-attacked from out of the forest. Before his men could help, the enemy had stabbed Thorolf with so many spears that he died there beside the forest.

It took a few moments for Egil to recover from the shock of this news, but rallying, he ran between the columns of his men and urged them to be brave. They regathered and followed him towards King Olaf the Red's column, and just as Thorolf had hoped, they were able to attack the enemy on their vulnerable side and inflicted heavy casualties. As many of King Olaf's men fled, King Athelstan had his standard brought forward and urged his men to launch an attack. Their assault was so fierce they broke the ranks of the Scottish king, who was killed along with many of his men. It was a great victory for King Athelstan.

Now, without saying a word, not even thank you, Egil accepts the invitation to take the high seat in front of King Athelstan. He casts his shield in front of his feet and takes the helmet from his head, laying down his sword across his knees. He knows he should have left his weapon and defensive armour outside, but right now he does not care about rules and etiquette. He is too angry at his brother's death, while the king and his men do not seem to care. To calm himself, he draws his sword halfway out of its sheath and then thrusts it back in. He does this again and again. Stopping suddenly and sitting upright, he keeps his head bowed. He does not want to look at anyone, especially King Athelstan.

Egil knows that his appearance and his actions must be making people around the king feel uneasy, even threatened. He has been told that when he is angry, the expression on his face becomes harsh and grim. And he is not a handsome man – he has a very broad forehead, bushy black eyebrows, a short and extremely wide nose, a broad chin with a jawbone covered by a long beard, a thick neck and broad shoulders – an appearance that is not only unappealing but also at times scary. His tall stature also makes him stand out. He had thick, wolf-grey hair when he was young, but went bald at an early age. Egil often wished he had taken after his mother's side of the family, like Thorolf, who was fair and handsome. But sometimes – like now – Egil is grateful for his ability to intimidate people with his appearance. He has even mastered how to raise and lower his bushy black eyebrows in turn to make people nervous, which he starts to do now, even with the king sitting directly in front of him. He begins to move his sword up and down again, all to demonstrate his great displeasure. Finally, one of the servants brings him a horn with mead, but he refuses to drink.

Because of his unusual appearance, it has been suggested that Egil suffered from Paget's disease, which is a chronic bone disorder. Normally, there is a process in which bones break down and then regrow. In Paget's disease, there is excessive breakdown and regrowth of bone, and because the bones regrow too quickly, they are bigger than normal, which can lead to deformities. Paget's disease of bone commonly occurs in the skull.

Egil keeps his head lowered, with his eyes hidden beneath his bushy eyebrows. The others do not realize he can still see what is going on around him. King Athelstan has his sword laid across his knees, and he is staring back at Egil. The king soon unsheathes his sword, one that Egil can recognize as very precious – single-bladed, about 30 inches long and made of pattern-welded high-carbon steel with silver alloy inlay and ornate designs on the pommel. There is an inscription inlaid on the blade that reads '+VFLBERHT' (meaning Ulfberth's sword – being of Frankish origin, this may refer to the blacksmith who first created one of these fine swords). Egil believes the blade was imported to Norway, possibly from the Rhineland.

The king takes a fine ring from his arm, slips it over the point of his sword, walks across the floor and calls to Egil to come over. Woken from his state of anger, Egil does not hesitate. He loves jewellery and fine metals and can never get enough of them. He is not surprised when the king hands the ring to him over the fire. Egil puts his sword through the ring, pulls it towards himself and then goes back to his place at the table. The king, too, sits down in his high seat. Egil examines the ring and can tell it is made of very fine gold. It is formed from a pair of twisted gold rods with a pair of twisted wires laid between them and the faces of dragons at either end. Egil is grateful for the gift. He knows an arm ring is not only decoration but also a token of status, wealth, loyalty, family, manhood and skill in battle. He draws it onto his arm. He loves the look of the ring. It immediately relaxes him, so he decides to stop moving his eyebrows, gently puts down his sword and helmet, takes the drinking horn that is now served to him, finishes it in huge gulps and asks for another.

Egil realizes it is time for him to say something, but he is a skald and finds it difficult to express his feelings except through poetry. He closes his eyes for a while to concentrate on composing a thank-you verse to the king for the arm ring. When he is done reciting, Egil can tell that King Athelstan is pleased with the verse, because he has two chests brought in, each carried by two men. The king tells the men to bring the chests to the high seat where Egil is sitting. He says, 'These chests, both full of silver, are yours, Egil. And if you go back to Iceland, I want you to present this money to your father as compensation for the death of his son. Please share some of

the money with Thorolf's kinsmen, the ones you like the best.
Take compensation for your brother from me here, either land
or wealth, whichever you prefer. And if you'd like to stay with
me longer, I'll grant you any honour and respect that you care
to name yourself.'

Egil opens the chests, takes out a few silver coins from
each, weighs them in his hand and looks them over carefully.
He can tell this is very good silver. He readily accepts the gift
and asks for another horn of mead. After drinking it, he again
closes his eyes to compose a poem to thank the king for his
gift and friendship. He speaks this verse:

> *For sorrow my beetling brows*
> *drooped over my eyelids.*
> *Now I have found one who smoothed*
> *the wrinkles on my forehead:*
> *The king has pushed the cliffs*
> *that gird my face*
> *back above my eyes.*
> *He grants bracelets no quarter.*

Egil eventually returned to Iceland, his native country,
and settled down with his two chests of silver. But greed
continued to consume him. He could not bring himself
to give any of the silver to his father or Thorolf's kinsmen,
keeping it all for himself. In his old age, Egil once again
gave vent to his contrariness and buried his treasure,
without revealing its hiding place to a single soul.

1ST HOUR OF THE NIGHT
(18.00–19.00)

A BOATBUILDER
FINISHES BUILDING
A SHIP

G rim Haraldsson goes back to look at his newly built
ship after a quick dinner with his wife, Kristin, and
their teenage sons, Harald and Thorbjörn. He knows his
family would have liked him to remain inside and keep them
company for the entire evening, but he is so close to finishing
the ship that he cannot tear himself away from this latest
project. Grim is aware that Olaf Thorsson, the young man
who commissioned him to build the ship, does not expect
him to finish it until the autumn, but the summer is coming
to an end quickly and Grim needs to take advantage of the
remaining daylight time. All too soon, the days will be much

shorter in Trondheim, where he lives very close to the coast. He is fortunate not to be living any further north, where the Norwegian winters start earlier and in mid-winter it is dark nearly all day and night.

Grim is a boatbuilder by trade. His speciality is small boats, which he makes primarily for the use of lake and river dwellers. Over the years, he has made many boats, especially one-person rowboats. For these, he begins by laying the keel, which is the bottom-most plank that runs the length of the boat. Then he adds two 'strake' planks immediately adjacent to the keel on each side, running lengthways from stem (the bow or front) to stern (at the rear). Three timbers are then fastened directly to this shell with trenails, which are wooden pegs driven into holes bored into the planks. Such a boat is rowed by a single person sitting amidships using a paddle, which he also fabricates. Grim himself owns three small boats – one for himself and two for his sons. Now that his sons are teenagers, they use them for fishing. When they were younger, he often took them to a nearby lake or river so they could paddle around just for fun. Grim has never relied on fishing to make a living – he has plenty to do as a boatbuilder – but Kristin is always pleased when their sons come home with salmon from the river.

Grim looks at the ship, which is stored on his land near his house, and is very pleased, even though building it has been a huge challenge. There have been times when he felt he was not up to the task after Olaf Thorsson arrived unexpectedly at his house one morning in the early spring, introduced himself and asked if Grim would build him a ship. While Grim felt flattered, he was taken aback. He told Olaf he was a boatbuilder and had never built a ship before. 'I'm not sure I can do it,' Grim said. 'It takes a lot of special skills that I may not have.' But this did not discourage Olaf. Instead, he said to Grim: 'I've heard a lot of good things about your boats. I'm sure you can find a way. Ask around, and maybe some other shipbuilders can advise you, though I know they're all very busy. That's why I'm coming to you.'

Before Grim had time to respond, Olaf opened his purse, took out a handful of silver and gave it to him. Grim's heart almost stopped. He had never seen so much fine silver in his life. He knew it would help him and his family get through the winter much more comfortably, so he wanted to accept the job – but he had one more question for Olaf. 'Before I agree to do this, what kind of ship do you have in mind?' In Olaf's response, Grim found out that the visitor knew exactly what he wanted – a 60- to 80-foot longship. 'I'd like it to be deep and wide in the beam. I don't need many oars, because I primarily plan on using the sail for propulsion.' Olaf did not tell Grim why he wanted this type of ship, but from these specifications, he speculated that Olaf wanted a cargo ship so he could try his luck as a trader.

Grim could see that the young man was not poor, so he

began to suspect that he had older brothers and that his family had no more heritable land for him. As Grim felt the weight of the silver in his hand, he became more reluctant to hand it back and finally said, 'Alright, I'll build you a ship, but please don't expect me to be done until autumn.' Olaf appeared relieved and said he was pleased. The pair shook hands to seal the deal, and Olaf told Grim where he lived in case he had questions. 'If I don't hear from you, I'll see you in the autumn.' With that, Olaf took off on his horse.

After Olaf had left, Grim sat down and began to calculate what he needed to build such a ship. He knew he would need lots of wood, which is required to make the hull (the watertight body of the ship), the trenails, the rudder used

THE REMAINS OF A VIKING LONGSHIP FOUND AT GOKSTAD
IN SOUTHERN NORWAY.

to steer the ship, as well as bailers, gangplanks and other equipment. He estimated he would need eleven trees, each approximately 3.3 feet in diameter and about 16 feet in length, as well as another tree, about 50 feet long, just for the keel. He summoned Harald and Thorbjörn. 'I've been assigned a big job,' he told them. 'I have to build a ship, and I need your help.' Fortunately, Grim has a fair amount of land, much of it forested with pine trees. He knows that oak is the preferred timber for shipbuilding, but where he lives oak is scarce. The three men immediately went to examine trees and began to mark the ones that seemed suitable.

Although Grim's two boys are the sons of a boatbuilder, neither had helped to build a ship before, so Grim started by sharing with them some of the basics. He described the parts of a ship and which bits must be made from curved timber – such as the stem, which stretches up from each end of the keel to the gunwale at the top edge of the hull, and the ribs, which resemble human ribs and stretch up from the keel all around the sides of the hull, also to the gunwale. He explained that straight-grained logs could be used for other parts, like the keel, planks, mast and crossbeams.

After they had felled the trees, they used hafted metal wedges or axes to split the logs lengthways into equal and uniform wedge-shaped planks called 'cloveboards', sometimes as many as sixteen from a log, then scraped them into the various shapes needed for the ship. For very long and wide planks and stringers, they split the trunk only in two and then shaped each half into a single plank. For beams and stringers, they needed to split a trunk into four sections. For other parts, like the keel and the stems, they might not need to split the logs at all but could cut them directly from a trunk. If a log was too hard to split, they could cut it in half to make things easier. If a timber ended up being too short, they could lengthen it with 'scarf' joints by cutting corresponding angles in two pieces of wood. They then had to work the ends of the fitting pieces to a sharp edge and join them. Grim explained that cuts for scarf joints must be sharp and clean so the pieces fit snuggly together, and that all these joints should face the aft or rear of the ship to minimize leakage.

This work took many weeks, even though Grim and his two sons worked from early morning until late evening. Grim was happy when this heavy part of the job was done, because Harald and Thorbjörn were beginning to complain about fatigue. One evening after dinner, Grim looked at his sons and could tell that the toll of the work had been hard on their bodies. He could never have done all the work by himself, so he went to his and Kristin's bedroom, opened the chest in which he kept the silver given to him by Olaf, and took out three pieces of silver. He went back to join his little family, sat down and gave each of his sons a piece of silver. 'This is payment for your hard work,' he said. The boys stared at him in surprise. Never before had they been paid for their work. Grim smiled when his sons no longer looked so exhausted. Then he turned to Kristin and asked her to hold out her hand. 'This is your reward for having done all the work in and around the house while we've been so busy,' he said, and put the third piece of silver in her hand. 'It is for you to spend on whatever you want.' Kristin beamed at him. Grim could tell that her mind immediately began to wander. A new dress, new decorative beads, new furnishings for their house?

Grim climbs onto the ship and looks around. In many ways, it is a traditional ship.

Conventional ships have a clinker-built hull of overlapping planks or strakes, which are fastened with iron nails. The top planks have an upward curve at the ends, which make the ship higher fore and aft than amidships. The bottom planks are attached to the slightly curved keel, which extends into the curved fore stem and after stem at the bow and stern. The outer

planks are attached to the ribs, which help to stabilize
the ship's shape and add stiffness to the shell, all made
from the naturally curved timbers harvested from
surrounding forests. The hull is further strengthened
with crossbeams placed across the width of the hull,
and floor timbers are attached to the planking. The
upper crossbeams can be used as rowing benches, with
the rower's feet resting on the lower crossbeams.

Because of Olaf's instructions, Grim has cut oar holes only at
the ends. Since there are so few, Grim decided not to bother
adding wooden covers for them. A rudder has been mounted
on the starboard side of the stern, so that during beaching this
steering oar, which extends below the keel, can be swivelled
upward and thereby raised, so it will not be damaged.

In the middle of the summer, Olaf had again showed up
unexpectedly, curious to see what progress Grim was making
on the ship. Grim was grateful for his visit, because he had
questions about what kind of mast he wanted. He explained
to Olaf that the mast is always slotted into a hole cut in the

keelson, a wooden structure resting on the keel to distribute the weight of the mast, and a 'mast partner', a heavy block of wood resting on the crossbeam, provides additional support. He told him that on some ships, this mast partner has a long opening that faces aft, so the mast can be lowered or raised at will without needing to be lifted vertically out of its socket. Olaf stared at Grim, like he did not understand what he was talking about, and it became obvious to Grim that Olaf knew very little about shipbuilding.

Eventually, Olaf said he did not need a mast that could be lowered or raised, because he mostly planned to use his ship to transport cargo to and from Kaupang, further south in Norway. Grim then asked Olaf about what kind of sail and anchor he was planning to use. 'You have to understand,' he said to Olaf, 'I only do the woodwork. I recommend that you look around for someone who can provide those to you. The anchors I know of are made of iron and T-shaped with curved arms that taper to the points.' Olaf nodded like he understood and rode off.

Grim is not only eager to be done with the ship because it will soon be autumn, but also because he is ready to get on with other projects. Over the summer, he received several orders for boats, as well as a request to build another ship. A man by the name of Erlend Jonsson, whom he did not know, had come to his house in the middle of summer, asking to see the ship he was building for Olaf. Grim thinks he got his name from Olaf, who seemed pleased when he came to see his ship's progress. He imagines that Olaf then told others in the district about his new shipbuilding skills. This time, however,

Grim did not readily agree to build Erlend a ship, saying instead that he will think about it. The silver he received from Olaf was indeed welcome, but the work on the ship had been very hard – physically and emotionally – on him, his wife and their two sons. For now, he thinks his family needs a rest from the stress of shipbuilding. Besides, there is no way he would want to try to build a ship during the winter months.

Grim sits down on one of the upper crossbeams and tries to imagine what it would be like to be the captain of this ship, or even a member of its crew, but the thought does not appeal to him at all. He likes his quiet life in Trondheim with his family and the occasional trip to the lakes and rivers in his small boats. Still, he is very proud of what he and his sons have accomplished in a short time. He checks that the strakes have all been fastened with iron nails. He knows he still needs to caulk them with tarred animal hair to make the hull watertight, and he also has to make the oars.

Suddenly, he realizes he has spent too much time sitting and pondering the life of a trader. He jumps down from the crossbeam and sees there is not enough sunlight left today to do any more work. Breaking into a smile, he mumbles, 'There's always tomorrow,' and goes inside to be with his family.

Olaf returned that autumn and expressed his pleasure with the ship. Again, he gave Grim a handful of good silver. Grim later learned that Olaf had become a successful trader buying walrus tusks and hides from further north and selling them in Kaupang.

A KING ATTENDS A SACRIFICIAL FEAST

King Hakon the Good Haraldsson is attending a sacrificial feast at Hladir in late autumn. He was invited months ago but was reluctant to accept the invitation because he is a Christian. Despite his many efforts, he knows that a large number of people in Norway still have not converted to Christianity. Many continue to sacrifice to the Heathen gods, as they do at this feast. But as the King of Norway, he realizes he cannot discriminate against pagans, on whom he depends for political support. So he agreed to show up, though he has been dreading this day.

At these sacrificial feasts, the guests drink huge quantities of mead and get very drunk. What is even worse, he knows, is that they often eat horse meat, which is against his religion. At past events like this, King Hakon made it a practice not to sit in the high seat. Instead, he would eat in the company of a few men in a little house away from the hall where the sacrificial feast took place. It was brought to his attention, however, that the farmers were complaining about his absence. Earl Sigurd Hakonarson, his close friend, warned him that he must stop this habit of eating separately. 'You may not like the food you are being served,' Sigurd said, 'but it is disrespectful not to join in and be with the people who support you and show you such cheerful hospitality.'

King Hakon has no idea what today's sacrificial feast is about, or for which god or gods. He suspects that the feast is in honour of a supernatural spirit that is supposed to grant a mild winter to these people at Hladir. Hakon has no recollection of pagan customs from his youth as he did not grow up with them. Although he was born in Norway as the youngest son of King Harald Fairhair Halfdanarson and had spent his early years there, his father sent him to the court of King Athelstan of England, where he was fostered. Back then, King Harald

Fairhair was trying to unify Norway, so he wanted to keep his son out of harm's way.

Hakon was later told that King Athelstan was tricked into fostering him by his father's envoy, who had placed the young Hakon on King Athelstan's knees. According to an old custom called 'knee-sitting', the English king was then obligated to formally adopt the boy. Today, King Hakon believes the story is just a rumour, but even if it were true, it never mattered to King Athelstan. Hakon had always felt welcome at the king's court. He treated Hakon well, provided him with an education, introduced him to Christianity and had him baptized. Upon the news of the death of Hakon's father, King Athelstan provided him with ships and men for an expedition against his half-brother Eirik Bloodaxe, who had just been proclaimed King of Norway. Hakon was to return to his homeland to challenge for his rightful place on the throne.

King Hakon now sits in the high seat and hopes that this evening's festivities will go as smoothly as those last evening – thanks to Earl Sigurd. Yesterday, when the first beaker was served, Earl Sigurd had proposed a toast dedicating the horn to Odin, and drank to the king. He then handed the horn to King Hakon, who accepted it and immediately made the sign of the cross over it before taking a draught. After he had finished his drink, someone yelled, 'Why did the king do that? Doesn't he want to drink out of the sacrificial beaker?' After a long silence, Earl Sigurd came to King Hakon's rescue, saying, 'The king has done as anyone who believes in his own might and strength would do. First, he dedicated his beaker to Thor. Then, over it, he made the sign of the hammer before drinking.' No one made further comments, though King Hakon could tell from some expressions in the crowd that not everyone was convinced by Earl Sigurd's explanation.

King Hakon is aware that the people in the crowd do not know that he secretly practises Christianity. Each week, he fasts on Fridays and observes Sundays. They do not know that he plans to make a law that their Yule celebration is to take place at the same time as the Christian custom of Christmas. His law will say that during the pagan Yuletide, everyone is to drink ale from a measure of grain or else pay a fine while the ale lasts.

Earl Sigurd has been a trusted and faithful friend for years. Their friendships dates to the time Hakon returned to Norway from England at the age of fifteen, and upon the advice of his friends and foster father he immediately sailed north to Trondheim to meet him. An exceptionally shrewd man, Earl Sigurd received him well, and the two soon entered into an agreement – if Hakon were to become king, he promised to give Earl Sigurd great power.

They then called together an assembly attended by many farmers. Earl Sigurd spoke on behalf of Hakon and counselled them to choose him as king in place of his half-brother, Eirik Bloodaxe. Hakon also gave a speech, asking for their support and that they stand by him. In return, Hakon promised to give up the rights of taxation over inherited property that had been claimed by his father. When they heard this, all began to call out: they wanted him to rule as king over the whole country.

With this wind in his political sails, Hakon assembled a bodyguard and, together with Earl Sigurd, took off on a royal campaign trip around the country. He received a warm welcome everywhere. Serving as his eyes and ears, Earl Sigurd told Hakon that people felt he was very much like his father, Harald Fairhair, with one important exception – his father had made slaves of all the people and had oppressed them, while Hakon wished everyone well and offered to return to the landholders the estates which his father had taken away.

Eirik Bloodaxe soon found himself alone, deserted by his followers. To save his own life and those of his family, he fled the country. He sailed first to Orkney, and then to England, where he would later meet a violent death at Stainmore in Westmorland.

After King Harald forced Eric Bloodaxe to abdicate, Eric raided in Scotland and around the Irish Sea until he was invited to become King of York by the Northumbrian Danes. Due to the opposition of the English King Eadrec, he was forced out and replaced by King Olaf Sihtricsson of Dublin. In 952, King Olaf was expelled and invited back. However, two years later he was ousted from York and killed at Stainmore.

Now, everyone is seated at the tables and drinking merrily. On this festive evening, no one questions why King Hakon makes the sign of the cross every time he takes a draught. When the meal is finally brought in, King Hakon sees to his horror – but not to his surprise – that it is horse meat, which he knows he cannot eat. He once asked King Athelstan why Christians are banned from eating horse meat. King Athelstan patiently explained to him that in the Bible it is told that prohibited foods include anything from animals that do not chew cud and do not have cloven hoofs. Hakon accepted the explanation, but then asked why Christians were permitted to eat pigs. To this, King Athelstan had no good answer. He simply responded that it must be that horses are associated with companionship, royalty and war. Pigs are not. The king also mentioned that a few centuries ago, the pope had instructed his subjects to stop eating horse meat because he considered it an impure and detestable pagan food, eaten only by Germanic peoples.

King Hakon looks at the horse meat on his plate and compares it with the cuts of meat on the plates of those around him. He has been told that the cuts of a horse are the same as those of a beef cow – the rear cuts are more tender, lean and tasty than the fore cuts, which are rich in connective tissue and take a long time to cook to tenderize. He knows that the hosts have gone out of their way to give him the best part of their horse. He believes it is from a newly slaughtered young animal, slaughtered to honour not only him but also the god or spirit for whom they are hosting this feast. King Hakon admits to himself that the smell is delicious. He is so hungry that he feels tempted to eat the slab of meat on his plate; he quickly says a silent prayer, asking God to forgive him for this temptation. He then strokes his long beard, stares at his plate and glances at Earl Sigurd, hoping his friend can help him again. But not this time, for Sigurd is busy chatting with the person seated next to him. With no other choice, King Hakon takes his eating utensils and moves the meat around on his plate, taking care not to have the meat touch the other foods. To satisfy his hunger, he begins to eat just the vegetables – boiled cabbage, boiled beets and fried onions.

He looks around at the farmers, who are eating the horse meat with their hands. 'These people have no manners,' he thinks to himself. He feels disgusted at the sight of their greasy mouths and fingers. One of the farmers, clearly in deep conversation with the man next to him, gestures wildly with a meat bone in his hand. The grease runs all the way down to his elbow.

After quickly eating the vegetables, King Hakon realizes he cannot fool the others into thinking he is leaving the meat on his plate because he has no appetite. He also knows he cannot move the meat to Earl Sigurd's plate without others noticing, because all farmers' eyes are on him now. Some throng around him and say that he absolutely must eat the wonderful horse meat on his plate. 'I refuse,' he says, finally. 'It is against my Christian faith. There is no way that I will eat it.'

Some men just laugh and shake their heads, but he can tell that many others are insulted. They begin to grow impatient with him. 'Come on, at least drink the broth from the meat,' one man says. Again, King Hakon refuses. Finally, the farmer who King Hakon believes is the owner of the estate and the host, asks him to drink the drippings from the meat. 'Under no circumstances,' King Hakon replies. 'I greatly appreciate your hospitality and your fine food, but do not ask me to do something that is forbidden to Christians.'

It becomes clear to him that the farmers are growing increasingly frustrated with his stubbornness. They do not understand why eating horse meat, which they relish, is forbidden to Christians. They think his adherence to Christian practices is exaggerated. They certainly do not comprehend the strength of his religious beliefs. With their annoyance growing, some farmers run up to the king, grab him and wrestle him out of his seat. Others try to force his mouth open and shove bits of horse meat with drippings into his mouth. King Hakon is desperate for Earl Sigurd's help. He thinks he has been abandoned, but he is relieved when he sees his friend stand up and shout to the crowd: 'Stop! Stop this!'

A VIKING AGE BRONZE KETTLE DECORATED WITH INTRICATE FACES. THESE REMAINS WERE FOUND IN WESTERN NORWAY.

Then Earl Sigurd adds calmly: 'I'll see to it that we can come to an agreement. I'm asking you all now to let go of our king and return to your seats.'

The men follow his request. King Hakon, shaking off the shock of the tumult, returns to his high seat. One of the farmers had choked him so hard he thought he might suffocate. Two others had tried so hard to pry open his mouth, he worried his jawbone might break. He can still feel and smell their greasy hands on his face, throat and arms. He cannot wait to rinse himself off in a nearby lake, cold though it will be.

King Hakon has no idea what Earl Sigurd has in mind now. But he has made up his own mind that he is willing to do just about anything to avoid another assault – except eat horse meat. Earl Sigurd asks King Hakon to please come forward to the table, where he has placed a kettle. He tells the king:

'When I tell you to, you'll open your mouth over the handle of the kettle. You can see that the handle is greasy where the smoke of the broth from the horse meat has settled.' King Hakon is confused and does not know what to do, but when Earl Sigurd winks at him he thinks that maybe his friend has found another solution.

He walks confidently to the kettle, where Earl Sigurd provides him with a linen cloth. King Hakon then puts the cloth over the handle and, as he has been directed, gapes with his mouth over the cloth for less than a minute. 'Is that it?' he can hear the farmers mumble to themselves. The king now looks around and can see that some farmers are not satisfied with Earl Sigurd's solution – but no one says anything, so King Hakon walks back to his high seat. 'Thank you,' he mouths to Earl Sigurd. It is over.

Years later, King Hakon won a final victory over Eirik Bloodaxe's sons in a battle at his own residence at Fitjar. Unfortunately, he also died in the surprise attack. He was laid to rest in the burial mound in the village of Seim in Lindås.

3RD HOUR OF THE NIGHT
(20.00–21.00)

A CHIEFTAIN IS
BURNED IN HIS HOUSE

Njal Thorgeirsson and his three surviving sons – Skarphedin, Helgi and Grim – as well as his son-in-law, Kari, have gathered with their male servants in front of Njal's farmhouse at Bergthorshvol. Together, they number almost thirty. They watch carefully as a large group of their enemies – Flosi Thordarson and his men – arrive and tether their horses in a depression on a nearby knoll. The size of Flosi's forces makes Njal very worried, so he directs all his men to go inside the house to join their spouses, children and the servant women. 'This house is solid,' he says confidently, 'so they won't be able to overcome us in there.'

But Skarphedin strongly objects to his father's plan to

retreat inside: it is better to stay here and fight them outside tonight. He argues that Flosi is desperate to end the feud here, because he and his men know it will be their deaths if they have to fight another day. 'Besides, going inside will only make us vulnerable to fire,' says Skarphedin, 'and Flosi is cowardly enough to burn the house down if he has the opportunity.' Helgi can tell that his father is very upset at Skarphedin's words and pleads with everyone to follow Njal's advice. Skarphedin reluctantly agrees. 'I'm ready to please him by burning in the house with him,' he says, 'for I'm not afraid to face my death.'

Once inside the farmhouse, however, Njal can see through the peephole that Skarphedin has not followed his instructions but has positioned himself with an axe, alone, at the front door. He watches as one of Flosi's men runs towards Skarphedin and lunges at him with a spear. Skarphedin quickly responds by hacking off the shaft of the spear and running at his opponent, wielding his axe. The blade crashes through the man's shield and hits him in the face, killing him instantly.

Helgi, Grim and Kari rush outside to help Skarphedin, attacking Flosi's men with spears and wounding many, who then retreat. In the long pause that follows, Njal assumes that Flosi, stunned by his sons' strong defence, must have realized that he and his men cannot win with their meagre weapons. They must be meeting about what to do next. That is when the truth of Skarphedin's predictions begin to become clear. Flosi has only two options available to him now – either turn back, which will eventually lead to the death of his men, or set fire to the house. It does not take long for Flosi and his men to decide. Soon, some of them return to start a blaze in front of each door.

Two of Njal's servant women are quick to act, however. They race to the storage room for vats of whey, which they pour on the flames to extinguish them. Njal hopes his enemies have now given up and retreated – but then he thinks he smells the smoke of burnt chickweed. He suspects that Flosi's men may have discovered the huge pile of chickweed at the back of the house and set that on fire. No one else seems to notice anything, until a little later some of the women and children complain about smarting eyes and begin to cough. They think the smoke is coming from the doused cooking fire, so a servant woman goes to check and reports that it is not the source.

All of a sudden, several people see flames falling down onto the hall and shout that the house is on fire. Flosi's men had indeed set the chickweed on fire, though not in the back, as Njal had predicted, but, much worse, in the loft above the crossbeams. Some now stand frozen, paralyzed with fear, not knowing what to do. Others try to run outside, only to find large fires again in front of all the doors. As the man of the house, Njal knows it is his duty to take control, to calm everyone down amid the commotion. He closes his eyes for a few seconds to collect his thoughts and, though the smoke is making him start to cough as well, he yells to get everyone's attention. 'Bear this bravely and do not be afraid,' he says, 'for this is only a brief storm and it will be a long time before we have another like it. Have faith that God is merciful. He will not let us burn, neither in this world nor in the next.' Njal goes around the house to offer words of comfort to those who are most upset.

Just now, Njal recalls the words of his wife, Bergthora, at dinner a few hours before, when she had encouraged everyone to eat their favourite foods – she had prepared fried lamb chops, wind-dried cod with butter, flatbread, cheese and a hot milk soup with mountain grass – and to eat a lot of it, as she announced that this would be the last evening she would be serving food. Everyone had looked at her in surprise and said that this could not be, but she claimed that if Grim and Helgi came home *before* they finished eating, this would be an omen that her announcement would come true. When she brought the food to the table, Njal remembers looking around and saying, 'Something strange is happening to me. I am having visions. I see both gable walls gone and the table and food all covered with blood.' He could tell from their silence that everyone felt ill at ease – all except Skarphedin, who calmly told people not to grieve and to be strong.

At that very moment, Grim and Helgi entered the house. They had spent the entire day at Holar, where their children were being fostered, and were not expected home that evening. Remembering Bergthora's words, everyone looked at the two brothers with alarm. Njal asked why they had returned in such a hurry and why so early. They reported that on the way, they had met some poor women and asked them for news. The women mentioned they had seen something unusual, and when the brothers insisted to know what it was, the women told them they had seen two groups of men in full armour riding in a hurry towards Thrihyrning Ridge. Helgi suspected Flosi was on his way to join the other men, so he decided that he and Grim should return and join their father and brothers at once. Njal remembers sighing deeply then; he knew his visions and Bergthora's premonitions were accurate. He told everyone not to go to bed that evening.

Njal had actually seen this disaster coming for a long time and had tried everything in his power to avert it. For many years, there had been a conflict between his sons and the family of Thrain Sigfusson. The dispute originated in Norway, where Thrain had distinguished himself at the court of Earl Hakon Sigurdarson. Njal's sons, Grim and Helgi, later joined Thrain in Norway, after they survived a Viking attack with the help of Kari Sölmundarson, an Icelander who had recognized their distinguished names. Then, another arrival, a man named Hrapp Örgumleidarson, joined the group in Norway and before long marked his presence by seducing Earl Hakon's daughter and killing his foreman, for which he was outlawed.

When Thrain and Njal's sons were about to set sail from Norway themselves, Hrapp hid on their ship and took passage with them. Earl Hakon, who suspected Njal's sons of complicity in hiding Hrapp, had them sized, but they managed to escape and take refuge with Kari, who negotiated a reconciliation with Earl Hakon and later returned to Iceland, where he married Njal's daughter, Helga. Grim and Helgi would not let matters rest, however, and sought compensation from Thrain for their arrest. When they were refused, and even insulted, they killed both Thrain and Hrapp. Further bloodshed was avoided for a while through the mediation of Thrain's brother, Ketil, who took it upon himself to foster his deceased brother's son, Höskuld.

To re-establish good relations with the Sigfusson family, Njal then assumed the duty of fostering Höskuld, whom he came to love as much as or maybe even more than his biological sons. When foster son Höskuld came of age, Njal betrothed him to Hildigun, Flosi's niece, and even managed to acquire a chieftainship for Höskuld to settle the marriage arrangement. Njal hoped then that the blood feud had finally come to an end – but the peace did not last long. It was soon rekindled when Thrain's relative, Lyting, killed Höskuld, and in return Njal's other three sons along with his grandson and Höskuld's son, Amundi, killed not only Lyting but also two of his brothers.

To add to Njal's problems, it turned out that the chieftainship he had established for Höskuld had cut into the constituency of another chieftain, Mörd Valgardsson. In retaliation, Mörd began to cultivate a friendship with Njal's three surviving biological sons in order to sow dissension between them and Höskuld. Every time his sons returned home rich with gifts from Mörd, Njal's heart would sink. Njal suspected they were jealous of his love for Höskuld. He knew that Mörd was slandering Höskuld and that his sons were foolish enough to believe Mörd. He was not particularly surprised when they eventually killed Höskuld, but Njal never forgave them.

'Tragic news and terrible to hear,' was Njal's reaction when Skarphedin told him about Höskuld's death. 'It is fair to say that I am so deeply touched with grief that I would rather have lost two of my sons, as long as Höskuld were still alive.' It was the saddest day in his life, and from then on he had a premonition that this killing would lead to the death of him, Bergthora and his remaining sons.

Later, when Njal and his sons rode to the Althing, he found that Mörd had prepared a prosecution against his sons. He also saw that Flosi was there and that he had some men assembled, no doubt incited by Hildigun, Flosi's niece, to take blood vengeance for the killing of her husband and

Njal's biological son Höskuld. Njal was not ready to give up, however, so he asked his sons to help him make the rounds of the chieftains, asking for their support. Unfortunately, Skarphedin turned people away with his sharp rejoinders, and Njal's plans for support did not work. As a last measure, he proposed mediation with Flosi for a settlement arranged by arbitrators, but Flosi and Skarphedin wrangled over the payment so much that, in the end, it came to nothing.

The whole house is now in flames. Njal battles his way outside and asks to speak with Flosi in the hope that his enemy will agree to a settlement with his sons, or at least let some of his people leave the house, but Flosi flatly refuses to make a settlement with Grim, Helgi and Skarphedin. 'Our dealings with them will soon be over, and we will not leave until they are dead,' he says. However, Flosi will allow the women, children and servants to come out.

Before she leaves, Thorhalla, Helgi's wife, promises that she will incite her father and brothers to take vengeance for the killings that are done. Then Astrid, Grim's wife, quickly devises a plan to save Helgi: 'Come out with me. I'll throw a kerchief over you and wrap another around your head, so that you look like a woman.' Helgi reluctantly agrees, but when he walks out with Astrid, Flosi is suspicious of seeing such a tall and broad-shouldered woman. He calls out to one of his men: 'Grab her and hold on!' Helgi takes offence of being referred to as a woman and throws off his kerchiefs. When he does, he is quickly killed.

After the servants, women and children have left the burning house, Flosi comes to the door. He tells Njal and Bergthora he wants to offer the couple a free exit, claiming that they do not deserve to be burned. 'I don't want to leave,' says Njal, 'because I'm too old to avenge my sons, and I don't want to live in shame.' Njal turns to his wife, hoping she will decide to accept Flosi's offer, but she refuses, saying she wants the same fate to await them both.

The couple goes back inside. Njal asks that they go to their bed and lie down. But then Bergthora notices with horror that the young boy, Thord, Kari and Helga's son, is still inside the house. She tells him that he will be carried out by someone, but the boy refuses. 'You promised me, Grandma, that we would never be parted,' he says, 'and I'd rather die with you.' She does not have the time or the energy to dissuade the stubborn boy, so she carries him to the bed to lie with her.

Njal tells his foreman where he, Berthora and Thord will be and that they have no intention of budging from the spot, no matter how much the smoke and fire may bother them. 'Now that you know where we are, that's where you can find our remains,' he tells him. Finally, he asks the foreman to spread the hide of a newly slaughtered ox over them when the three of them are in the bed. With the boy between them, Njal and Bergthora cross themselves and then the boy. When the hide is over them, Njal closes his eyes.

Njal and his family succomb in the flames. Only Kari, Njal's son-in-law, escapes and later manages to kill several of the arsonists. Towards the end of their lives, Flosi and Kari both seek absolution in Rome.

A WOMAN
TAKES UP ARMS

A ud mounts her horse, her dependable brown companion who has always served her so well. To make her ride more comfortable, she is wearing breeches rather than a traditional woollen dress. She keeps on her linen chemise, which she tucks into her breeches, but leaves behind her scarf and the belt with her knife, purse and keys to her treasury chest. It is late summer, and Aud decides she does not need her sleeved cloak either, even though it is starting to get a little cooler in the evenings. Besides, the rage she is feeling inside her belly will keep her warm.

All she carries is a short-sword, which she found among the belongings of her ex-husband, who had been so quick to

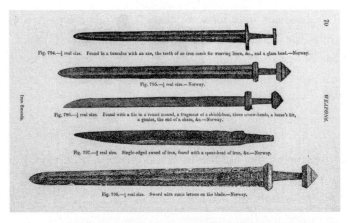

AN ILLUSTRATION OF SOME EXAMPLES OF VIKING AGE SWORDS OF DIFFERING SIZES, ALL MADE FROM IRON.

divorce her he had not even bothered to take all his clothes and weapons. For all she knows, the breeches she is wearing had belonged to him, too, but she does not really care. Not now. She just wants to ride as light as possible because she is in a hurry to complete a mission, a carefully laid-out plan that she developed over the summer. She flies from her home at Hol at such speed that her farmhand, a boy who looks after the ewes and whom she has asked to ride with her, can barely keep up.

Aud has been irate for some time. In fact, she has come to truly hate Thord Ingunnarson, her ex-husband, for what he has done to her. About a year ago, without warning, Thord publicly declared himself divorced from her at the Althing. She received the humiliating news from her two brothers when they returned from the assembly. Thord had not been man enough, thought Aud, to invite her to the Althing and tell her in person, nor had he ever bothered to tell her he was unhappy in their marriage.

Admittedly, she had not been completely surprised by the news. She and Thord had merely coexisted for some time, with little affection between them. Aud even began to suspect he was having an affair with Gudrun Osvifsdottir, who had been married to an elderly rich man named Thorvald. Thord would often ride over to Gudrun and Thorvald's farm at Laugar and sometimes would not come home until very late at night or early in the morning. Thord said his frequent visits were to see Thorvald, but despite his immense riches, Thorvald was not highly regarded in the district, and Aud could not imagine why Thord would be interested in his company. No, she began to realize, he went there to see Gudrun. She knew that Gudrun did not love Thorvald, that she had been married to him against her will at a very young age and purely for his wealth. She also heard rumours from people in the neighbourhood that Gudrun had made her husband a shirt with the neck so low it showed his nipples. After he wore the ridiculous shirt, she claimed it as proof that Thorvald had become demented or was somehow sexually deviant and used it as an excuse to divorce him.

The reason Thord gave for divorcing Aud at the Althing was equally ridiculous. He claimed she had taken to wearing breeches with a codpiece, like a masculine woman. It is true that on a couple of occasions she had taken off her mid-calf woollen dress and borrowed her husband's breeches, simply to do her outside chores more easily, especially when she had to ride a horse for any distance. Aud suspected that Gudrun, a crafty woman, was behind this silly accusation.

Aud can understand why Thord would be attracted to Gudrun, however. Though spend-thrift, she is a young, charming, beautiful, intelligent woman who comes from a distinguished family. Aud knows she cannot complete with Gudrun in appearance – she does not have Gudrun's slender figure, feminine curves, long blonde hair or interest in finery and fancy clothes. She seldom bothers to wear her tall, attractive headdress. The only jewellery she owns are the festoons of glass beads hanging on straps between the brooches that hold together her shoulder straps when she does wear a dress. She sometimes second-guesses herself that perhaps if, on occasion, she had dressed up and made more of an attempt to look appealing to her husband, she might have saved their marriage.

But when she and Thord married, she had hoped he would appreciate and even love her for being such an efficient and accomplished housewife. Like many married women in

Iceland, Aud oversaw most indoor work, including preserving and preparing the food and drink, cleaning the house, manufacturing the cloth and producing the garments and wall hangings. Spinning was especially laborious, though sometimes Thord had helped out. Because of the large size of their farm and the small number of farmhands and female workers, Aud also had to work outdoors to collect berries, mosses, herbs, seaweed, wild fruit and birds' eggs. In addition, she was the one who washed the clothes in local streams and fetched water for drinking, cooking and bathing.

Unfortunately, and much to her regret, she had been unable to conceive and so the couple remained childless. She knows Thord wanted a child, preferably a son, but she had never managed to become pregnant. Aud admits, too, that she had never truly loved Thord, though she admired him for his remarkable skills in law and found him handsome with his tall stature and black hair and beard. Like so many other young women in Iceland, Aud was not asked for her opinion when Thord approached her father to ask for her hand in marriage. Thord had simply arrived at her father's house, and her father had found him acceptable. She had been absent, too, during follow-up negotiations between the two men, though she knows that Thord had paid a reasonable bride price and that her father had agreed to hand over her dowry, the sum of her inheritance, at the wedding. Aud remembers she was not annoyed with her father for not consulting her. In many ways, she considered herself lucky to be given to Thord in marriage. For years, the two had got along, for the most part, rarely arguing, and he had never been physically or verbally abusive.

But today is different. After her divorce, Aud expected her brothers to take revenge for the public insult to her honour. As a woman in Iceland, she has no legal rights. She cannot serve as a chieftain or a judge, cannot be a witness and cannot speak at assemblies. She knows that if a woman wants to initiate or conduct legal proceedings, a man has to do so on her behalf – by law, she is under the authority of her male relatives. Her father passed away some years ago, and of course she has no grown son, so her two brothers are her legal guardians. She knows they were very displeased with her divorce. In fact, they had attempted to start a legal case against Thord, but they were unable to get sufficient support from others in the district to take the case further.

That is why Aud has decided to take matters into her own hands. She has no other choice. From the farm at Hol, she rides southwards over Saelingsdale Heath and does not stop until she reaches the wall of the hayfield at Laugar, where Thord is now living with Gudrun. It has been a fairly easy ride, even though it is evening. She and the horses only had to navigate around a few lava rocks, and because it is summer there is no snow to create hazardous crevasses. At the hayfield, she dismounts and tells the farmhand to look after the two horses. She carefully walks the short distance to the house.

She enters through the unlocked door, then steps into the fire hall and sees the bed closet ahead, where she knows Thord will be sleeping. The door is closed but not latched, so she slowly and quietly enters, seeing that Thord is sleeping on his back, a convenient position for what she intends to do now.

She knows that in Iceland it is the law that you must wake a man before you kill him. Killing a man in his sleep is called murder and the punishment is likely outlawry.

To slay someone was considered dishonorable murder only if it was not immediately made public or if it was committed under the cover of the dark of night. Evidently, it was regarded as obligatory to wake a sleeping enemy before one made an attack upon him, but in practice this was often just an empty gesture. The intended victim was often not given a chance to put up a real defence.

She touches Thord's shoulder to wake him up, but he just grunts and turns over on his side. She is not quite sure what to do next, for it is more difficult to kill a man lying this way. She takes a deep breath, draws her short-sword high above Thord and strikes him, leaving a great wound on his right arm and a gash across his chest. She is so strong that the force of her blow lodges the blade into the wood of his bed. She wastes no time removing it, then turns and flees back through the house, runs to her horse, jumps into the saddle and rides off together with the farmhand.

Once on her way, she slows down to take time to think about what she has done. She is annoyed that her plan to kill Thord, which she had plotted for weeks, did not work out exactly as she had wanted. Her scheming had started earlier in the summer, while she and others from Hol were staying at the shieling with the milking ewes in Hvammsdale.

A shieling is a hut or collection of huts on a seasonal pasture for cattle high in the hills or mountains. They were common in wild or sparsely populated areas.

At the same time, people from Laugar, where Thord was living, had taken their ewes to a shieling in Lambadale. Though the two communities are in separate valleys, only a single ridge divides them. Since the distance is not great and the ride not difficult, Aud asked her farmhand to do some detective work for her. Whenever he met with his counterpart from Laugar, a shepherd, he was to find out who was staying at the shieling in Lambadale and who had stayed back home at Laugar. To eliminate any suspicion, she instructed the farmhand to speak of Thord only in very friendly terms. When the farmhand reported back, she learned that Thord was busy building a new hall at Laugar with Gudrun's father, Osvif. Everyone else, including Thord's new wife, was staying in the shieling. That is why Aud has chosen today to strike.

When Aud finally returns home at sunrise, her brothers are waiting for her. They have been up all night worrying about her and wondering where she has gone. After she tells them the whole story, they say they are pleased and that Thord deserved even worse.

Later Aud heard from others in the district that it had taken Thord a long time to recuperate from his wounds.

The injuries in his chest healed well enough, but he never regained much use of his right arm. Aud knew she would be a suspect and expected Thord to prosecute her, but he did nothing in retribution and turned out to be a gentleman in the end. When, a year or so later, Thord was drowned at sea with his companions in a terrible storm, Aud's hatred turned to sadness as she mourned the death of her ex-husband. Nevertheless, she would never forgive Gudrun for stealing her husband.

5TH HOUR OF THE NIGHT
(22.00–23.00)

A DAUGHTER PREVENTS HER FATHER FROM COMMITTING SUICIDE

Thorgerd Egilsdottir lies comfortably in her bed across the room from that of her father, Egil Skallagrimsson, in the family's farmhouse at Borg. She is trying to rest in the bed closet, a warm and cosy private sleeping area partitioned off from the rest of the house. Thorgerd is exhausted, but she takes time now to scan her sleeping quarters and admire what her mother, Asgerd, has done to the room. The wall hangings are not only beautiful as decoration but also functional as insulation. The woollen blankets and furs on the bed are of the highest quality. Thorgerd is not surprised at her mother's fine work. She has always been such an exemplary homemaker, Thorgerd remembers, even when she was younger and living there with her parents long before she was married off.

Thorgerd is happy finally to get some rest after her long ride today, but she can tell that her father is sad. He lies flat on his back with his eyes closed and his arms folded stiffly across his chest. He does not utter a sound. She is concerned and has been working on what to say and do. She turns over, tosses her long dark hair to one side and rests her head in her hand. She tries to study her father, though the room is only dimly lit from a single lamp of soapstone on the floor of the bed closet. She can see there is but little oil left in the lamp.

Thorgerd and Egil live on separate farms a distance apart, so she has not seen her father for a while. As she observes him now, she finds it hard to believe how much he has aged. His long beard is completely grey. Even in this poor light, she can make out the many scars on his face, arms and hands that lie uncovered on his chest, marks that prove he has fought in many brutal battles in his long life. She has always known him as a fine family man, a good husband to his wife and a devoted father to his five children. But he is no longer the big, strong strapping man, so tall in stature, that she once knew and admired. She can see him now for what he has become – old, frail and tired.

She is surprised at how much he has changed. It is true that the death of his brother, Thorolf, in battle in England was hard on him, though that was a long time ago. 'Surely he has recovered from that,' she thinks. And since Thorolf's death,

Egil has made a good life for himself in Iceland, thanks in part to all the booty he brought home to Iceland from his Viking expeditions and in part to his inheritance of this farm at Borg. It has been many years since he last went on a Viking raid, And Thorgerd knows something else has aged him and made him depressed: the recent deaths of two of his sons.

Gunnar died a few months ago, and Thorgerd could not attend the funeral because of bad weather. She is not even sure what Gunnar died of, though she suspects it was a sudden illness. And now, her other beloved brother, Bödvar, has died just as suddenly. Bödvar was the eldest of Egil's three boys and Egil's favourite. The two were very attached and similar in important ways. Bödvar was big and strong like Egil and showed exceptional promise. She believes that Egil had planned for Bödvar to take over and inherit the farm at Borg one day. Fortunately, Bödvar did not inherit his father's looks, including Egil's enormously large head. No, Bödvar resembled Thorolf, his fair and handsome paternal uncle. But none of that matters now. Bödvar is gone, too. Egil has only his wife, his two daughters, Thorgerd and Bera, and his youngest son, Thorstein, left.

Thorgerd was her parents' first born. She and her father have always got along well because their personalities are so much alike – both silent and strong-willed. Thorgerd has always been grateful to her father for marrying her off to Olaf Höskuldsson, a wealthy and handsome man of a distinguished family. Olaf's mother, Melkorka, was the daughter of King Myrkjartan of Ireland. When Thorgerd married Olaf, Egil provided them with a huge dowry as her contribution to the new household. Thanks to Olaf's wealth and Egil's generosity, she has never lacked for anything.

Thorgerd was at home with her husband this morning, at their farm at Hjardarholt, when a messenger arrived. He announced that her mother, Asgerd, was asking her to come to Borg as soon as possible because Egil had locked himself in his bed closet. The messenger explained that people had knocked again and again on his door, but her father would not come out. He had taken neither food nor drink for three full days, and no one dared to speak to him. 'Why? What on earth happened?' Thorgerd asked the messenger. He then gave her the full story.

Egil had bought a load of timber from a Norwegian ship moored at Hvita River. Egil then assigned Bödvar and some men from his household to fetch the wood and bring it back to his farm at Borg. Bödvar and Egil's farmhands rode their horses to Vellir, from where they were to set off for Hvita River in Egil's eight-oared vessel. The trip was doomed from the start. They only had a crew of six, not eight, to manoeuvre their ship. Then, just as they were ready to set off, their departure was delayed until late evening by a high tide in the afternoon. When they finally took off, a wild south-westerly wind arose. The sea in the fjord soon turned turbulent and the ship sunk beneath the waves. The following day, bodies began washing ashore, the messenger told.

Thorgerd cried, 'Oh, what dreadful news! How many of them drowned?' When the messenger reported that there were no survivors, she choked back her tears and only managed a whisper: 'Was my brother's body found?' The messenger said yes, all had been recovered. Then she asked, 'How is my father taking this?'

Thorgerd learned that upon hearing the awful news, Egil immediately rode off to search for the bodies. He found his son. Bödvar's remains had drifted ashore at Einarsnes. Some of the other drowned victims were found further south, where their doomed ship had also made land. It was reported, said the messenger, that her father picked up Bödvar's body, mounted his horse and placed his son's corpse across his knees. From there, Egil rode to Digranes, where his own father, Skallagrim, lay buried in a mound. Eyewitnesses said that Egil opened the mound, laid Bödvar next to Skallagrim, his grandfather, and closed the mound again. Egil was working until sunset.

The messenger had more interesting details. 'People say that when Egil buried Bödvar, Egil was wearing tight-fitting hose and a tight red fustian tunic laced at the sides,' he told Thorgerd. 'But when he placed Bödvar in the mound, the tunic and hose burst off the body. That's what they say, but I cannot verify this.' Then he added, 'What I do know for certain is that when Egil came home, he went straight to his bed closet, locked his door from the inside and has been there ever since.' After hearing this, Thorgerd quickly saddled her horse and, together with the messenger, rode hard on the long trip from Hjardarholt to Borg.

Now, Thorgerd finds herself staring at her father in his bed. It is well into the night. She knows what Egil intends to do – take his own life. But during her long ride here today, she had time to devise a way to prevent her father's suicide. It is a clever plan.

The ruse started as soon as she and the messenger arrived that evening. She knew that her mother, true to her good nature, would ask as soon as they entered the door: 'Did you have a meal on the way? Are you hungry?' Her response was swift and loud, so loud her father would hear her, even in his bed closet. 'I have eaten nothing and want nothing. I just want to die and go to Freyja.' She said she wanted to join her father in his death. 'I don't want to live after my father and two brothers are dead.'

Her plan was in motion. She could see her mother shaking her head. Thorgerd went to the door of Egil's bed closet and called out to him: 'Open the door, father! I want both of us to go the same way.' Thorgerd knew Egil would unfasten his door and let her in. He praised her and said, 'My dear daughter, thank you for wanting to follow your father. You have shown great love for me. How can anyone expect me to live with such great sorrow?' Thorgerd looked back at her mother, who understood what her daughter was up to. Although grief-stricken and mourning the death of her son, Asgerd couldn't help but roll her eyes at her headstrong daughter. Thorgerd winked back to assure her that everything would turn out alright.

Egil now turns on his side to face Thorgerd. He clearly senses that she is looking at him. She is ready to employ the rest of her plan. 'What are you doing?' he says to her. 'Are you chewing something? We're supposed to starve ourselves to death, you know.' 'It's seaweed,' she replies. 'It's supposed to be bad for me, make me feel worse. Otherwise, I'm afraid I might live too long. I want to die with you.' She asks Egil if he would like some. 'OK,' he says. 'I'll take some. It can't hurt. It can only speed up my death, too.' She takes some out of her bag and gives it to him. She can soon hear him chewing and chewing. Thorgerd turns in her bed to face the wall away from her father. She does not want him to see her smiling, for she knows what is about to happen.

Soon she breaks the silence in the room. She calls out for someone to bring her some water. When she hears the knock on the door, she rises to unlock it. She takes the animal horn of drink that is brought to her. Then Egil says, 'Well, I suppose that's what happens when you eat seaweed. I found out it makes you thirsty.' Thorgerd bites her tongue to keep from laughing. 'It's working, it's working,' she thinks to herself. She does her best to look sombre and sad, then says to Egil: 'Would you like a drink, Father?' Without waiting for his response, she passes him the horn. He is dying of thirst and takes such a huge draught he almost empties it before he realizes what it is. 'This is not water!' he yells. Thorgerd takes the horn and drinks what little is left. 'You're right, father. It's milk. We've been tricked!'

Egil grabs the horn, bites off a huge chunk, then in disgust he throws it against the door. He leans back in his bed and lets out a huge sigh. The room grows quiet again, until Thorgerd says, 'Let's face it, Father. Our plan to starve ourselves to death has failed. What shall we do now?' Egil does not answer her.

So, Thorgerd proposes a new idea: they should both stay alive long enough for Egil to compose a poem in Bödvar's memory. 'I'll then carve the poem onto a rune stick,' she says. Not surprisingly, she has conveniently got both the stick and the knife she will need with her. 'I know the runes,' she adds, 'because you taught them to me when I was young. After that we can decide if we want to die or not.' Egil still does not answer, though she can tell she has his attention. She continues, 'If we die now, I doubt that Thorstein would ever compose a memorial poem to his brother or have a feast in his name. Who will honour Bödvar's memory, if not us?'

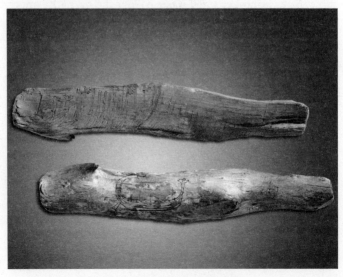

A PAIR OF RUNE STICKS LIKE THAT INTO WHICH THORGERD CARVES A POEM.

Egil finally speaks: 'I don't think I can compose a poem even if I try, but I'll give it my best.'

Thorgerd warmly hugs her father, unlocks the door and walks out. 'It worked,' she tells her mother, quietly. 'Now I'm ready for that meal. Seaweed is just not very filling.'

The next morning, Egil came out of the bed closet while Thorgerd and Asgerd were eating their morning meal. Both could tell he was in better spirits. He sat down in his high seat and delivered his poem to them. He called it 'The Loss of My Sons'. This is the first stanza of the poem:

My tongue is slow
for me to move
my poem's scales
laborious to rise.
Poetry is beyond
my grasp,
tough to drag out
from what is in my mind.

Later, Egil held a funeral feast. When Thorgerd decided to ride home later in the day, Egil gave her precious parting gifts. As she rode away, she thought her father's life was the most precious gift.

6TH HOUR OF THE NIGHT
(23.00–00.00)

A MAN BREASTFEEDS
A BABY

Thorgils Thordarson is sitting on a stool made from driftwood in his desolate hut in Greenland, watching over his newborn son. To keep the baby warm, he has wrapped the child in some of his own tattered clothes, then placed a seal skin over the top. Now, Thorgils picks him up and cradles him in his arms. He gently rocks back and forth, back and forth, to try to soothe his little boy, but it does little good. The infant continues to cry from hunger. If he is not fed soon, Thorgils worries, he will die. But what can Thorgils do? His wife and the boy's mother, Thorey, died after giving birth. Only he and a handful of his men are here to hear the baby's desperate cries. There is not even a cow or a goat that could be milked. But he knows even that would be useless; a newborn cannot digest milk from an animal. His son needs a human's breastmilk.

Thorgils has suffered much in his life. He has endured the loss of friends and family members over the years, and now his beloved spouse. But the death of his latest child would be too much sorrow to bear, he tells his men. He vows to do anything to save him.

Thorgils is a Christian. He was one of the first men in Iceland to receive the new faith. But his conversion to Christianity was difficult and came at a cost. The pagan god Thor, whom he once worshipped, would not forgive him. He began to harass Thorgils in his dreams. It started one night when Thor appeared to him with an evil look on his face. The god accused Thorgils of betrayal. The next morning, he woke up to find that his hayfield boar was dead. The following night, Thor reappeared in his dream and this time threatened to kill more of his livestock. And indeed he did, for Thorgils learned the next day that his old ox had died. By the third night of Thor's hauntings, Thorgils decided he had had enough. He made up his mind to stay awake all night with his cattle. Surely then, he thought, nothing could happen to them. But Thor thought of another way to exact his vengeance. Thorgils has no recollection of what happened during the night or how, but when he returned to his farm in the morning, his body was black and blue. His household could only speculate that he must have been in a fight with Thor.

Thorgils has always lived a good and pure life. For this, he believes, his Christian God rewarded him well, because back in Iceland he had been a very successful and powerful man in his community. His faith was strong then, and it sustained him. But here now in Greenland, holding his starving baby, he feels his Christian faith weakening. He starts to question God's own goodness and to wonder if God is truly fair and righteous. 'How can you do this to me?' he says loudly, with his head raised towards the ceiling of the hut.

He regrets coming to live in Greenland. 'How foolish of me,' he moans. He remembers when Eirik the Red, the first Norse settler in Greenland, started sending messages to Iceland inviting him to take his pick of the best land available. Thorgils had ignored those fine offers until his son, Thorleif, who was then twenty years old, arrived on a ship from Greenland and told him many wonderful things about the newly settled country. Eventually, Thorgils discussed the possibility of emigrating with his wife, but she was reluctant. 'I think it's a bad idea to go there,' she said. 'But I'll go if you go.' Thorgils arranged for a caretaker to manage his property in Iceland and set about recruiting people to go with him. Thorleif eagerly said yes. And of course, he would take his slaves. A number of several close family members agreed, too.

Thorgils enlisted his foreman, whom he would need to help set up a farm in the new land. Another Icelandic family, headed by the farmer Jostein of Kalfaholt, decided to join them as well. Finally, Thorgils was ready for the journey. He bought a ship in Leiruvog, where they loaded their cargo, including farm animals, provisions and timber. Then, they waited for fair winds.

What a terrible journey to Greenland it turned out to be. Thorgils had expected Thor to disappear from his dreams as soon as he decided to leave Iceland. But as Thorgils was waiting to embark on his trip, the red-bearded god tested him again. 'This journey will not go well for you,' Thor warned him, 'unless you believe in me again.' In his dream, Thorgils told Thor go to away. He said the journey would go as Almighty God willed it.

When they finally set sail out of the fjord and lost sight of land, the winds died down again. They were at the whims of the calm sea for so long they began to run out of both food and water. His crew members became so desperate they suggested they drink their own urine just to get some liquid.

Thorgils would have none of that. Instead, he said, they would gather some rainwater from the ship's sail. Soon after, Thor appeared to Thorgils in a dream once more, saying, 'Hasn't it gone as I predicted?' Thorgils drove the god away with harsh words, though he was worried.

Autumn was drawing nearer, and his travel companions were becoming more and more desperate. Some encouraged him to invoke Thor, but he refused. Thorgils was not surprised when Thor reappeared in his dreams a couple of nights later, this time for his unwillingness to call upon him. Thor told him that he and his ship would never reach harbour, unless Thorgils gave him a gift. But what gift, Thorgils pondered. What could possibly please a vengeful god like Thor? Then Thorgils remembered that years before, when he was still a Heathen, he had dedicated to Thor the ox that was now onboard. The next morning – much to the dismay of his crew – he threw the ox overboard. Thor finally stopped haunting Thorgils, and they could proceed.

Just before winter set in, they were shipwrecked on the gravel in a bay beneath the glaciers of Greenland. No lives were lost, the livestock were saved and the ship's boat, which they had towed behind them, remained intact. Using driftwood found on the beaches, they built a hut with a single dividing wall. Thorgils' and Jostein's families took one side each. Most of the livestock quickly died from the cold and the lack of grass, so the men resorted to hunting and fishing for food. Thorgils worked harder than anyone because his wife was pregnant. He wanted to make sure she got sufficient nourishment.

Soon after their arrival in Greenland, however, a sickness

came over Jostein's family. Many of them died. No one knew what kind of sickness it was or from where it had come. It started with vomiting, then a mild fever, body aches and fatigue. Towards the end, the illness affected the brain. The sick went out of their minds and death was almost a relief. Eventually, the sickness spread to Thorgils' household and some of them died, too.

Still, there was something even worse than all these deaths: all the dead returned as ghosts to haunt the living. Most of the ghostly appearances took place in Jostein's side of the house, but no one suffered more than Thorgils, who was now visited in his dreams not by Thor but by the ghosts. Thorgils decided to gather all the corpses, which he had buried in the gravel near their hut, and burn them on a pyre. Finally, after all the bodies were reduced to ashes, the ghosts disappeared.

Now, Thorgils tries to digest the horrors of today, and Thorey's death most of all. He recalls a conversation he had with her a few months ago when she told him about a dream she'd had the night before, in which she saw a beautiful land and shining people. 'I think we may be delivered from these troubles,' she had said. At the time, Thorgils had mixed feelings about the dream. What if the Eden she envisioned referred not to some place in this world but in the other world? Could the dream be a premonition that she was going to die? Thorgils did not share his suspicions. He did not want to scare her. 'Have no worries,' he'd said instead. 'You've good things in store for you. The saints will help you, because you have lived a clean life.' After a long pause, she asked if he could possibly seek a way out of this wilderness. Thorgils did not know what to say to Thorey. He thought hard about an answer but eventually decided to be honest with her. 'No, at this point I cannot see a way.'

That was a couple of months ago. Since then, the weather had slowly improved, and this morning Thorgils decided to walk up onto the glacier with his men, to see if the ice had broken up enough that they could escape by boat. Thorey, who was very close to giving birth, stayed in bed. She pleaded with her husband not to leave her. He assured her that he and the other men would not be gone long and would only go a short distance away. He also told her that the slaves would have to row out to go fishing today. The foreman, he said, would see the slaves off and then come back and stay beside her, so she would not be alone.

The climb up the glacier was not bad. Thorgils carried a wood axe and was girded with his sword. By mid-afternoon, however, the weather had turned ugly, with heavy snow and strong winds. It got so bad that he told his team: 'We have to go back to the hut now.' Thorgils walked in front and was able to find the path back to the hut despite the blinding snow. It was late in the evening when they finally got back, but there was still a little daylight. When they reached the hut, they were surprised to find that the boat was nowhere to be seen. At first, they assumed the slaves were still out fishing and delayed because of the awful weather – but when they entered the hut, they knew something was terribly wrong. 'Something evil is going on here,' Thorgils said to his men in panic, for they found that not only were all the chests with their valuables and provisions gone, but so were his foreman and all the slaves. They walked further into the hut, then heard a gurgling sound coming from Thorey's bed. To their horror, they saw that she had given birth and was now dead. Her newborn son, starving for milk, was suckling at her lifeless body. Thorgils was horrified at the sight of his dead wife, and in panic he grabbed the baby while the others examined Thorey. They found a small wound under her arm, as if she had been stabbed with a slender-bladed knife. Everything on the bed was covered in blood.

Thorgils bitterly regrets leaving his wife's side this morning. But it is too late now to reflect on things he should not have done. He is still exhausted from his climb up the glacier and the strenuous trip back through the heavy snow. He looks at the infant in his arms, then lifts his feet and sets them on a block of wood. He asks one of his men to put hot embers near his feet, to warm them and keep him from falling asleep with the baby, who has now stopped crying and only whimpers in his arms.

'I don't see how this little boy can live much longer,' Thorgils says to his men. No one says a word, so Thorgils continues, 'I'll never forgive myself if I don't try to help him.' What he says next startles the men. 'First, I have to cut off my nipples,' he explains, as his men step back in horror. 'There's no time to explain,' he says, as he hands the baby to the closest man. He takes off his coat and tunic, grabs his razor-sharp knife, and sits back down, bare-chested, on the stool. With two swift slices, he removes his nipples and tosses them on the floor. Most of the men cannot bear to watch, but he does not care. Thorgils quickly begins to press hard on what little fat he has left around his breasts, which have become sunken from the lack of food and harsh living conditions over the winter. He manages to squeeze out some blood first, then, after a while, a mixed fluid. Thorgils keeps pressing and pressing. Finally, life-saving milk begins to flow. Thorgils takes his baby boy back into his arms and nurses the infant, who drinks hungrily and happily. The men are in awe, Thorgils in tears.

Thorgils is able to keep his son alive. He and his men
manage to fashion a boat out of hides with wooden
supports inside it. When the ice breaks up, they find a
way out and make it to Seleyrar by summer.

About the author

Kirsten Wolf is the Torger Thompson Chair of Scandinavian Studies in the Department of German, Nordic, and Slavic at the University of Wisconsin–Madison, where she teaches Old Norse-Icelandic language and literature and Scandinavian Linguistics. She has edited several Old Norse-Icelandic works and written books on the Vikings and the Viking Age. Her books on the Vikings comprise: *Vikings: An Encyclopedia of Conflict, Invasions, and Raids* (with Tristan Mueller-Vollmer, 2022), *The Vikings: Facts and Fictions* (with Tristan Mueller-Vollmer, 2018) and *Daily Life of the Vikings* (2013). Kirsten holds a PhD from University College London.

PICTURE CREDITS

The publisher would like to thank the following sources for their kind permission to reproduce the pictures in this book.

p. 187   Rischgitz/Getty Images

p. 203   Arild Finne Nybø via Flickr

p. 216   PhotoStock-Israel/Alamy Stock Photo

p. 232   Universitetsmuseet i Bergen, Fotoarkiv CC BY-SA
           4.0

All other illustrations provided by Shutterstock.

All maps drawn by David Woodroffe.

Every effort has been made to acknowledge correctly and contact the source and/or copyright holder of each picture and the publisher apologises for any unintentional errors or omissions, which will be corrected in future editions of this book.

Sources

7th hour of the night (00.00–01.00)

'Gisli Surson's Saga' (tr. Margin S. Regal and ed. Vidar Hreinsson) in *The Complete Sagas of Icelanders, including 49 Tales, Vol. 2* (Reykjavík: Leifur Eiríksson Publishing, 1997), pp. 1–48.

Peter Hallberg, *The Icelandic Saga* (tr. Paul Schach) (Lincoln: University of Nebraska Press, 1962).

8th hour of the night (01.00–02.00)

'Egil's Saga' (tr. Bernard Scudder and ed. Hreinsson) in *The Complete Sagas of Icelanders, including 49 Tales, Vol. 1* (Reykjavík: Leifur Eiríksson Publishing, 1997), pp. 33–177.

Snorri Sturluson, *Heimskringla: History of the Kings of Norway* (tr. Lee M. Hollander) (Austin: University of Texas Press, 1964).

The Poetic Edda (tr. Carolyne Larrington) (Oxford: Oxford University Press, 1996).

9th hour of the night (02.00–03.00)

Margaret Cormack, '*Fyr kné meyio*: Notes on Childbirth in Medieval Iceland', *Saga-Book of the Viking Club, Vol. XXV* (Exeter: Short-run Press Ltd, 2001), pp. 314–15.

Verena Höfig, 'Birth, Belts, and the *Bristinamen*', *Viking and Medieval Scandinavia*, vol. 15 (2019), pp. 127–50.

Jenny Jochens, *Women in Old Norse Society* (London: Cornell University Press, 1995).

'The Saga of Hord and the People of Holm' (tr. Robert Kellogg) in *The Complete Sagas of Icelanders, Vol. 2*, pp. 193–236.

10th hour of the night (03.00–04.00)

Peter Foote and David M. Wilson, *The Viking Achievement: The Society and Culture of Early Medieval Scandinavia* (London: Sidgwick & Jackson, 1970).

Tristan Mueller-Vollmer, 'Coins and Mints' in *Vikings: An Encylopedia of Conflict, Invasions, and Raids* (Santa Barbara: ABC-CLIO, 2022), pp. 75–7.

Kirsten Wolf, *Daily Life of the Vikings* (Westport: Greenwood Press, 2004).

11th hour of the night (04.00–05.00)

Paulus Orosius, *The Seven Books of History against the Pagans* (tr. Roy J. Deferrari) (Washington DC: Catholic University of America Press, 1964).

Foote and Wilson, *The Viking Achievement*.

Wolf, *Daily Life of the Vikings*.

12th hour of the night (05.00–06.00)

'Eirik the Red's Saga' (tr. Keneva Kunz) in *The Complete Sagas of Icelanders, Vol. 1*, pp. 1–18.

The Vinland Sagas: The Norse Discovery of America (tr. Magnus Magnusson and Hermann Pálsson) (Harmondsworth: Penguin, 1965).

'The Saga of the Greenlanders' (tr. Keneva Kunz) in *The Complete Sagas of Icelanders, Vol. 1*, pp. 19–32.

1st hour of the day (06.00–07.00)

Jenny Jochins, 'Old Norse Motherhood' in *Medieval Mothering* (ed. John Carmi Parsons and Bonnie Wheeler) (New York: Garland, 1996), pp. 201–22.

'The Saga of Hord and the People of Holm' (tr. Robert Kellogg) in *The Complete Sagas of Icelanders, Vol. 2*, pp. 193–236.

2nd hour of the day (07.00–08.00)

Tristan Mueller-Vollmer and Kirsten Wolf, *Vikings: An Encylopedia of Conflict, Invasions, and Raids* (Santa Barbara: ABC-CLIO, 2022).

3rd hour of the day (08.00–09.00)

'The Saga of the People of Eyri' (tr. Judy Quinn and ed. Hreinsson) in *The Complete Sagas of Icelanders Including 49 Tales, Vol. 5* (Reykjavík: Leifur Eiríksson Publishing, 1997), pp. 131–218.

E. O. G. Turville-Petre, *Myth and Religion of the North: The Religion of Ancient Scandinavia* (New York: Holt, Rinehart and Winston, 1964).

4th hour of the day (09.00–10.00)

Einar Haugen, *The Scandinavian Languages: An Introduction to their History* (London: Faber & Faber, 1976).

R. I. Page, *Runes: Reading the Past* (London: British Museum
   Publications, 1987).

5th hour of the day (10.00–11.00)
Ari Thorgilsson, *The Book of Icelanders (Íslendingabók)* (tr.
   Halldór Hermansson) (Ithaca: Cornell University Press;
   London: Oxford University Press, 1930).
Njördur P. Njardvik, 'Birth of a Nation: The Story of the
   Icelandic Commonwealth', *Iceland Review*, 1973.

6th hour of the day (11.00–12.00)
'The Saga of the People of Laxardal' (tr. Keneva Kunz) in *The
   Complete Sagas of Icelanders, Vol. 5*, pp. 1–120.

7th hour of the day (12.00–13.00)
Preben Meulengracht Sørensen, *The Unmanly Man: Concepts
   of Sexual Defamation in Early Northern Society* (tr. Joan
   Turville-Petre) (Odense: Odense University Press, 1983).
'Njal's Saga' (tr. Robert Cook and ed. Vidar Hreinsson) in
   The Complete Sagas of Icelanders, including 49 Tales, Vol. 3.
   (Reykjavík: Leifur Eiríksson Publishing, 1997), pp. 1–220.

8th hour of the day (13.00–14.00)
Orkneyinga saga: The History of the Earls of Orkney (tr. Hermann
   Palsson and Paul Edwards) (London: Hogarth, 1978).

9th hour of the day (14.00–15.00)
'Kormak's saga' (tr. Rory McTurk) in *The Complete Sagas of
   Icelanders, Vol. 1*, pp. 179–224.

10th hour of the day (15.00–16.00)

Jochens, *Women in Old Norse Society*.

'Njal's Saga', pp. 1–220.

11th hour of the day (16.00–17.00)

Árni Björnsson, 'Icelandic Feasts and Holidays: Celebrations, Past and Present', *Iceland Review*, 1980.

Sidra Durst, 'Hákarl' in *They Eat What? A Cultural Encyclopedia of Weird and Exotic Food from Around the World* (ed. Jonathan Deutsch with Natalya Murakhver) (Santa Barbara: ABC-Clio, 2012), pp. 91–2.

Nanna Ragnvaldsdóttir and Michael R. Leaman. '*Thorrablót* – Icelandic Feasting' in *Celebration: Proceedings of the Oxford Symposium on Food and Cookery, 2011* (ed. Mark McWilliams) (London: Prospect Books, 2012), pp. 277–83.

12th hour of the day (17.00–18.00)

'Egil's Saga', pp. 33–117.

1st hour of the night (18.00–19.00)

Wolf, *Daily Life of the Vikings*.

2nd hour of the night (19.00–20.00)

Snorri Sturluson, *Heimskringla: History of the Kings of Norway* (tr. Lee M. Hollander) (Austin: University of Texas Press, 1964).

3rd hour of the night (20.00–21.00)

Theodore M. Andersson, *The Icelandic Family Saga: An Analytic Reading* (Cambridge: Harvard University Press, 1967).

'Njal's Saga', pp. 1–220.

4th hour of the night (21.00–22.00)

Jochens, *Women in Old Norse Society*.

'The Saga of the People of Laxardal' (tr. Keneva Kunz) in *The Complete Sagas of Icelanders, Vol. 5*, pp. 1–120.

5th hour of the night (22.00–23.00)

'Egil's Saga', pp. 33–117.

6th hour of the night (23.00–00.00)

'The Saga of the People of Floi' (tr. Paul Acker) in *The Complete Sagas of Icelanders, Vol. 3*, pp. 271–304.

Bibliography

KEY TEXTS CONSULTED BY THE AUTHOR

Andersson, Theodore M. *The Icelandic Family Saga: An Analytic Reading.* Cambridge, MA: Harvard University Press, 1967.

Thorgilsson, Ari. *The Book of Icelanders (Íslendingabók).* (Edited and translated by Halldór Hermannsson). Islandica 20. Ithaca: Cornell University Press; London: Oxford University Press, 1930.

The Complete Sagas of Icelanders Including 49 Tales. General editor Vidar Hreinsson. 5 vols. Reykjavík: Leifur Eiríksson Publishing, 1997.

Foote, Peter, and David M. Wilson. *The Viking Achievement: The Society and Culture of Early Medieval Scandinavia.* London: Sidgwick & Jackson, 1970.

Hallberg, Peter. *The Icelandic Saga.* Translated with Introduction and Notes by Paul Schach. Lincoln: University of Nebraska Press, 1962.

Sturluson, Snorri. *Heimskringla: History of the Kings of Norway.* Translated with Introduction and Notes by Lee M. Hollander. Austin: University of Texas Press, 1964.

Mueller-Vollmer, Tristan, and Kirsten Wolf. *Vikings: An Encyclopedia of Conflict, Invasions, and Raids.* Santa Barbara: ABC-CLIO, 2022.

Orkneyinga saga: The History of the Earls of Orkney. Translated by Hermann Palsson and Paul Edwards. London: Hogarth, 1978; rept. Harmondsworth: Penguin, 1981.

Roesdahl, Else. *Viking Age Denmark*. Translated by Susan M. Margeson and Kirsten Williams. London: British Museum Publications, 1982.

Roesdahl, Else. *The Vikings*. Translated by Susan M. Margeson and Kirsten Williams. London: Penguin, 1991.

Turville-Petre, E.O.G. *Myth and Religion of the North: The Religion of Ancient Scandinavia*. New York: Holt, Rinehart and Winston, 1964.

Wolf, Kirsten. *Daily Life of the Vikings*. Westport: Greenwood Press, 2004.

RECOMMENDED FURTHER READING

Brink, Stefan, in collaboration with Neil S. Price, eds. *The Viking World*. London: Routledge, 2012.

Brøndsted, Johannes. *The Vikings*. Translated by Kalle Skov. London: Harmondsworth, 1965.

Haywood, John. *Encyclopedia of the Viking Age*. New York: Thames and Haywood, 2000.

Magnusson, Magnus. *Vikings!* New York: E.P. Dutton, 1980.

Sawyer, P.H. *The Age of the Vikings*. 2nd edition. London: Edward Arnold Ltd, 1971.

Winroth, Anders. *The Age of the Vikings*. Princeton: Princeton University Press, 2014.

Wolf, Kirsten, and Tristan Mueller-Vollmer. *The Vikings: Facts and Fictions*. Santa Barbara: ABC-CLIO, 2018.

Names

Flosi Thordarson
Freydis Eiriksdottir
Geirmund Ingjaldsson
Gest Oddleifsson
Gilli the Russian
Gisli Sursson
Gissur Teitsson
Grim Njalsson
Grim Thorgeirsson
Grimkel Bjarnarson
Gudrun Osvifsdottir
Gunnar Egilsson
Gunnhild Özurardottir
Hakon Eiriksson
Hakon the Good Haraldsson
Hakon Sigurdarson
Hall Thorsteinsson
Harald Fairhair Halfdanarson
Harald Greycloak Eiriksson
Harald Hardruler Sigurdsson
Harald Maddadarson
Helga
Helga Njalsdottir
Helgi Njalsson
Hildigun Starkadsdottir
Hjalti Skeggjason
Hörd Grimkelsson
Höskuld Kolsson

Höskuld Thrainsson
Hrapp Örgumleidarson
Hrut Herjolfsson
Ingirid Thorkelsdottir
Ingun Thorisdottir
Jorun Bjarnardottir
Jostein of Kalfaholt
Kalf Arnfinsson
Kari Sölmundarson
Ketil Sigfusson
Kimbi
Kolbein Egilsson
Koll Kjallaksson
Kormak Ögmundarson
Leif Eiriksson
Ljot Hallsson
Lödmund Ulfsson
Lyting
Melkorka
Mörd Sighvatsson
Mörd Valgardsson
Myrkjartan
Njal Thorgeirsson
Olaf Feilan Thorsteinsson
Olaf Haraldsson
Olaf Höskuldsson
Olaf the Red
Olaf Sveinsson

Olaf Tryggvason

Ölvir

Osvif Helgason

Ottar

Runolf Ulfsson

Sigmund

Sigmund Özurarson

Signy Valbrandsdottir

Sigurd Gunnhildarson

Sigurd Hakonarson

Skallagrim Kveldulfsson

Skarphedin Njalsson

Skeggi Sinna-Bjarnarson

Snorri Thorbrandsson

Snorri Thorgrimsson

Steingerd Thorkelsdottir

Steinvör Hallsdottir

Surt Asbjarnarson

Svein Asleifarson

Særeif

Thangbrand

Thorbjörg Coal-brow

Thorbjörg Grimkelsdottir

Thorbrand Snorrason

Thorbrand Thorfinsson

Thord Arndisarson

Thord the Coward

Thord Ingunnarson

Thord Karason

Thordis

Thordis Sursdottir

Thorey Thorvardsdottir

Thorfin Karlsefni Thordarson

Thorgeir Thorkelsson

Thorgerd Egilsdottir

Thorgils Ögmundarson

Thorgils Thordarson

Thorgrim Thorkelsson

Thorgrim Thorsteinsson

Thorhalla Asgrimsdottir

Thorleif Thorgilsson

Thorir

Thorir the Hound

Thorkel of Tunga

Thorkel Sursson

Thormod Bersason

Thorodd Thorbrandsson

Thorolf Bjarnarson

Thorolf Skallagrimsson

Thorstein Egilsson

Thorstein Shipbuilder

Thorvald Halldorsson

Thorvard of Gardar

Thorveig of Steinsstadir

Thrain Sigfusson

Torfi Valbrandsson

Tosti
Unn Mardardottir
Valbrand Valthjofsson
Vestein Vesteinsson
Vidhugsi
Yaroslav of Novgorod

FICTIONAL NAMES

Asbjörn Jensson
Erlend Jonsson
Grim Haraldsson
Hans Jensson
Harald Grimsson
Harald Jensson
Jensina
Kristin
Olaf Ottarsson
Olaf Thorsson
Sigmund Arnason
Sigrid
Sigrid Steimgrimsdottir
Thorbjörn Grimsson

INDEX